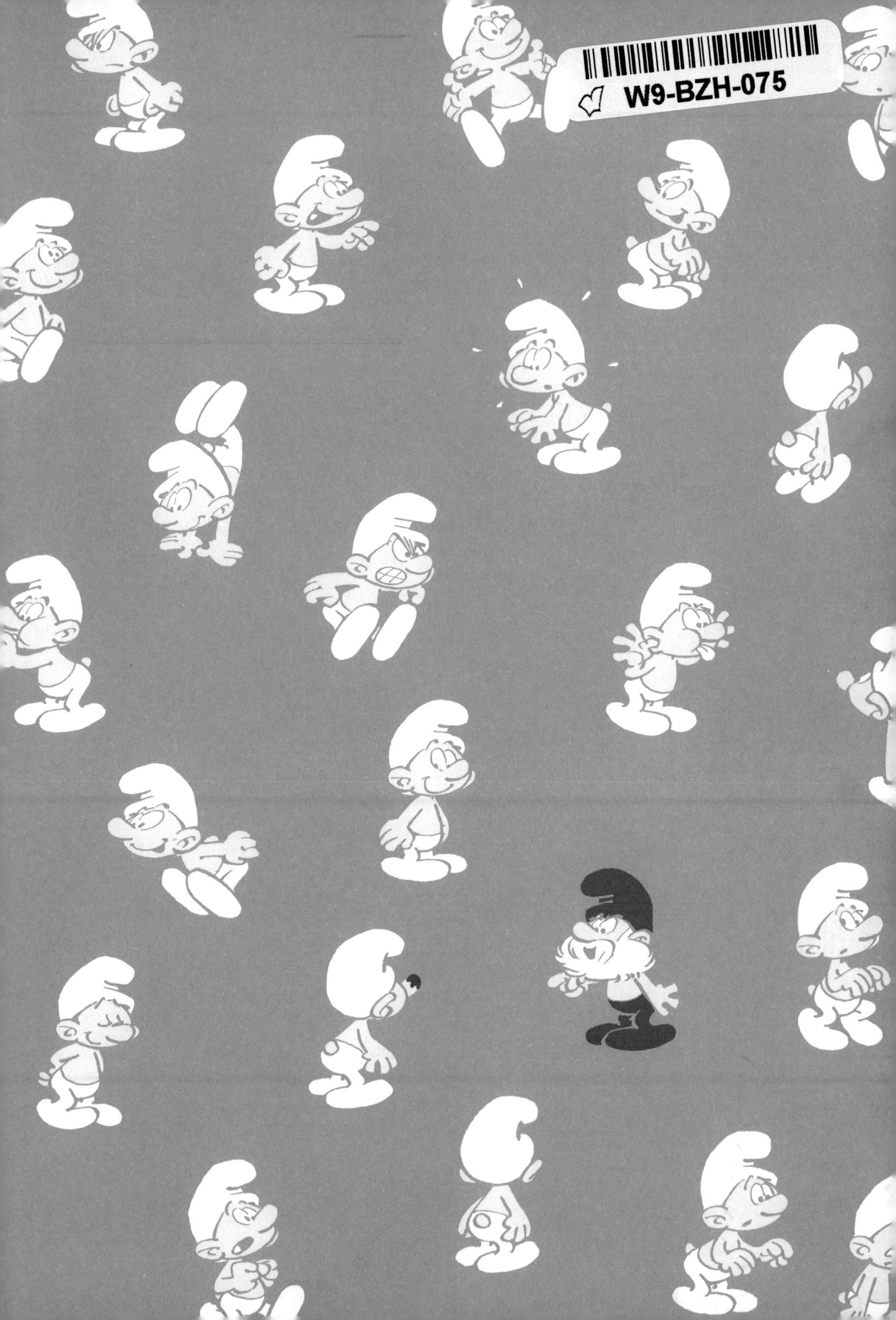

THE SMURF OLYMPICS

Peyo

THE SMURF OLYMPICS!

Here! Try to smurf it as far as possible!
Okay!
Whoa, it's heavy!
OUCH!
I'm sorry!
Hmm! It's okay...! Go ahead! Throw!
UHN!
!
WUMP
10

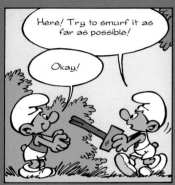

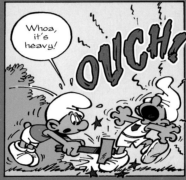

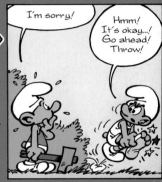

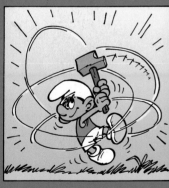

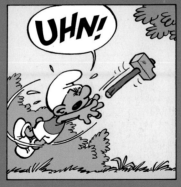

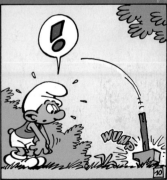

A SMURFS GRAPHIC NOVEL BY Peyo

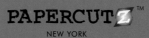

PAPERCUTZ™
NEW YORK

SMURFS GRAPHIC NOVELS AVAILABLE FROM PAPERCUTZ™

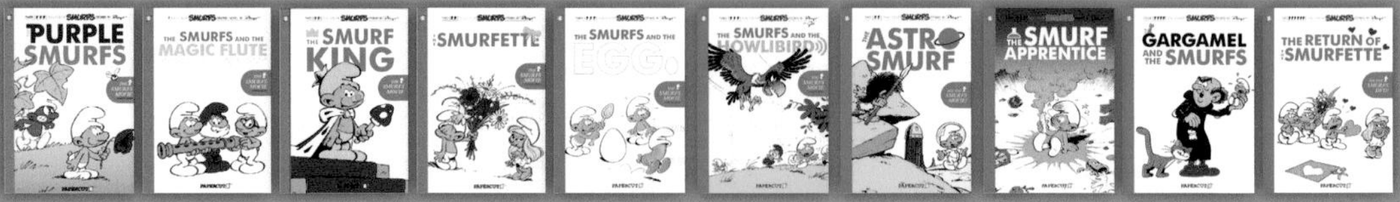

PURPLE SMURFS
THE SMURFS AND THE MAGIC FLUTE
THE SMURF KING
SMURFETTE
THE SMURFS AND THE EGG
THE SMURFS AND THE HOWLIBIRD
ASTRO SMURF
THE SMURF APPRENTICE
GARGAMEL AND THE SMURFS
THE RETURN OF THE SMURFETTE

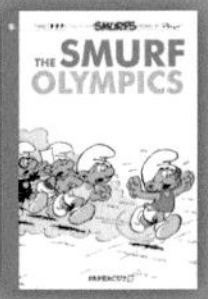

THE SMURF OLYMPICS

1. **THE PURPLE SMURFS**
2. **THE SMURFS AND THE MAGIC FLUTE**
3. **THE SMURF KING**
4. **THE SMURFETTE**
5. **THE SMURFS AND THE EGG**
6. **THE SMURFS AND THE HOWLIBIRD**
7. **THE ASTROSMURF**
8. **THE SMURF APPRENTICE**
9. **GARGAMEL AND THE SMURFS**
10. **THE RETURN OF THE SMURFETTE**
11. **THE SMURF OLYMPICS**

COMING SOON:

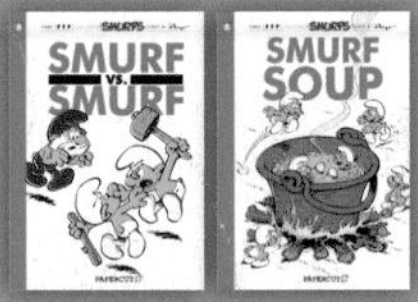

SMURF VS. SMURF
SMURF SOUP

12. **SMURF VS. SMURF**
13. **SMURF SOUP**

THE SMURF OLYMPICS

"The Smurf Olympics"
BY PEYO

"More Smurf Olympics"
BY YVAN DELPORTE AND PEYO

The Smurf Comic Strips
BY PEYO

"Smurf Vs.Smurf" Preview
BY YVAN DELPORTE AND PEYO

Joe Johnson, *SMURFLATIONS*
Adam Grano, *SMURFIC DESIGN*
Janice Chiang, *LETTERING SMURFETTE*
Matt. Murray, *SMURF CONSULTANT*
Michael Petranek, *ASSOCIATE SMURF*
Jim Salicrup, *SMURF-IN-CHIEF*

PAPERBACK EDITION ISBN: 978-1-59707-301-1
HARDCOVER EDITION ISBN: 978-1-59707-302-8

PRINTED IN CHINA APRIL 2012 BY WKT CO. LTD.
3/F PHASE I LEADER INDUSTRIAL CENTRE
188 TEXACO ROAD, TSEUN WAN, N.T., HONG KONG

DISTRIBUTED BY MACMILLAN
FIRST PAPERCUTZ PRINTING

Peyo

THE SMURF OLYMPICS

THE SMURF OLYMPICS

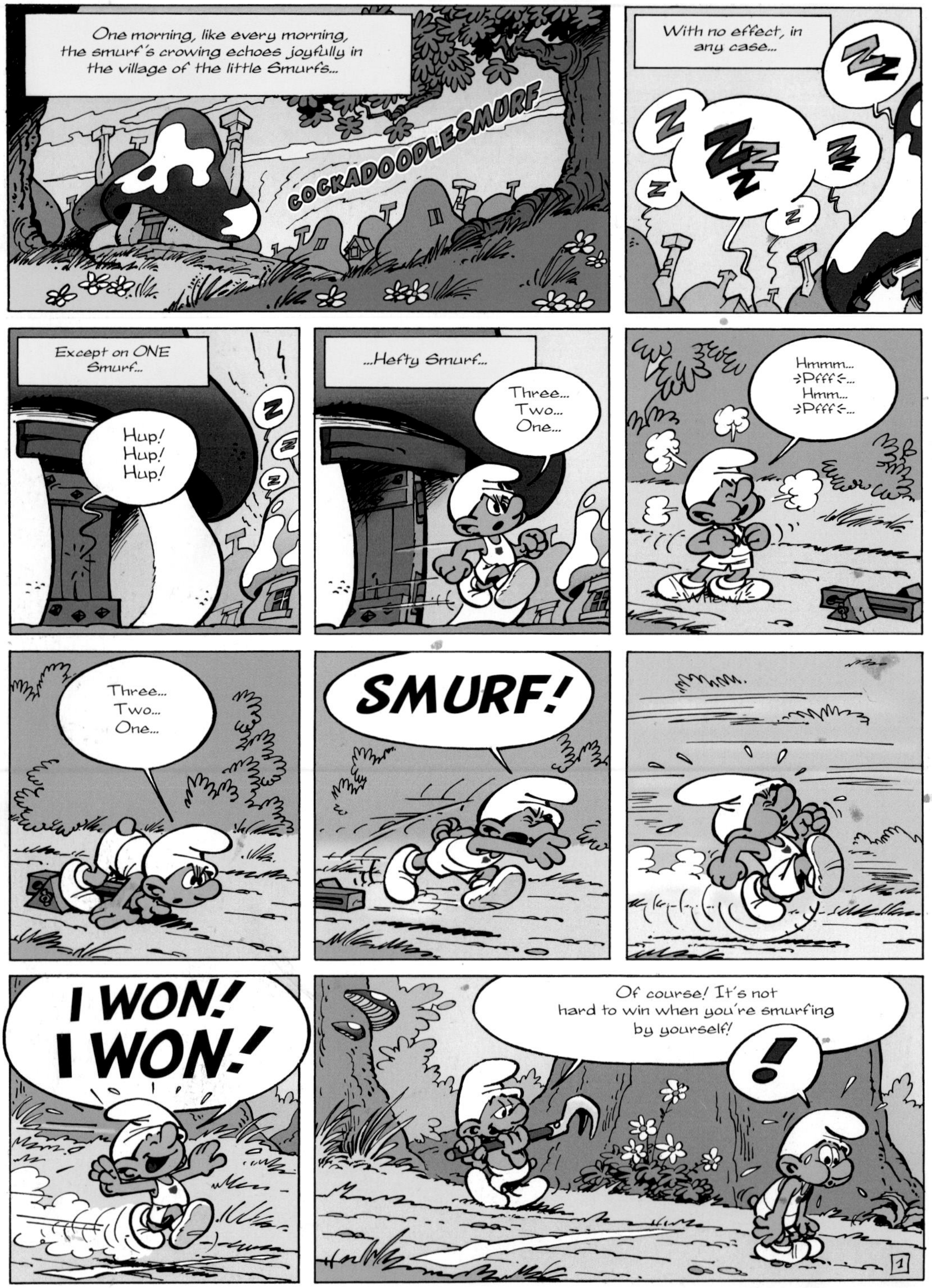

One morning, like every morning, the smurf's crowing echoes joyfully in the village of the little Smurfs...
COCKADOODLESMURF
With no effect, in any case...
Except on ONE Smurf...
Hup! Hup! Hup!
...Hefty Smurf...
Three... Two... One...
Hmmm... Pfff... Hmm... Pfff...
Three... Two... One...
SMURF!
I WON! I WON!
Of course! It's not hard to win when you're smurfing by yourself!
!
1

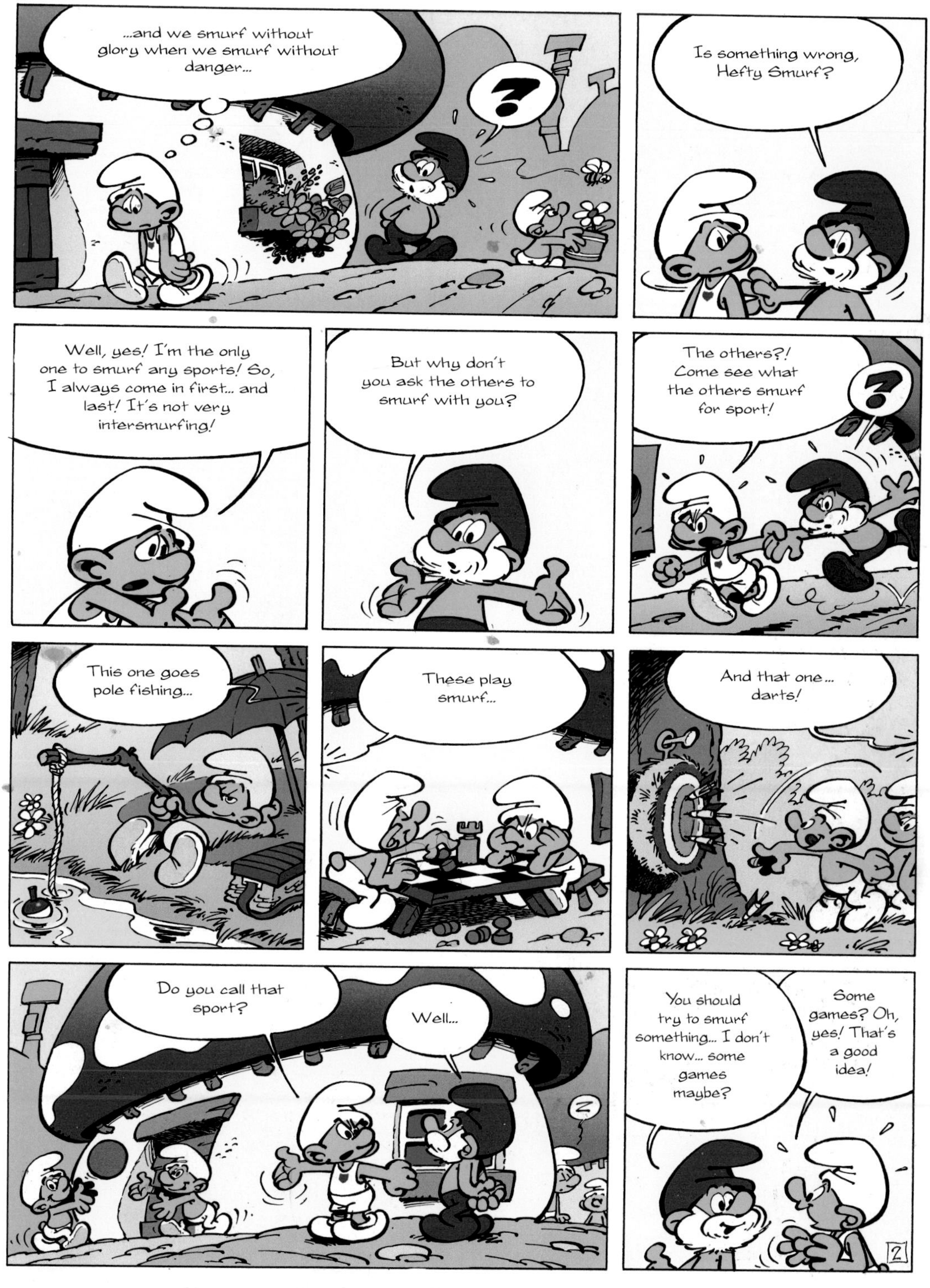
...and we smurf without glory when we smurf without danger...
?
Is something wrong, Hefty Smurf?
Well, yes! I'm the only one to smurf any sports! So, I always come in first... and last! It's not very intersmurfing!
But why don't you ask the others to smurf with you?
The others?! Come see what the others smurf for sport!
?
This one goes pole fishing...
These play smurf...
And that one... darts!
Do you call that sport?
Well...
Z
You should try to smurf something... I don't know... some games maybe?
Some games? Oh, yes! That's a good idea!
2

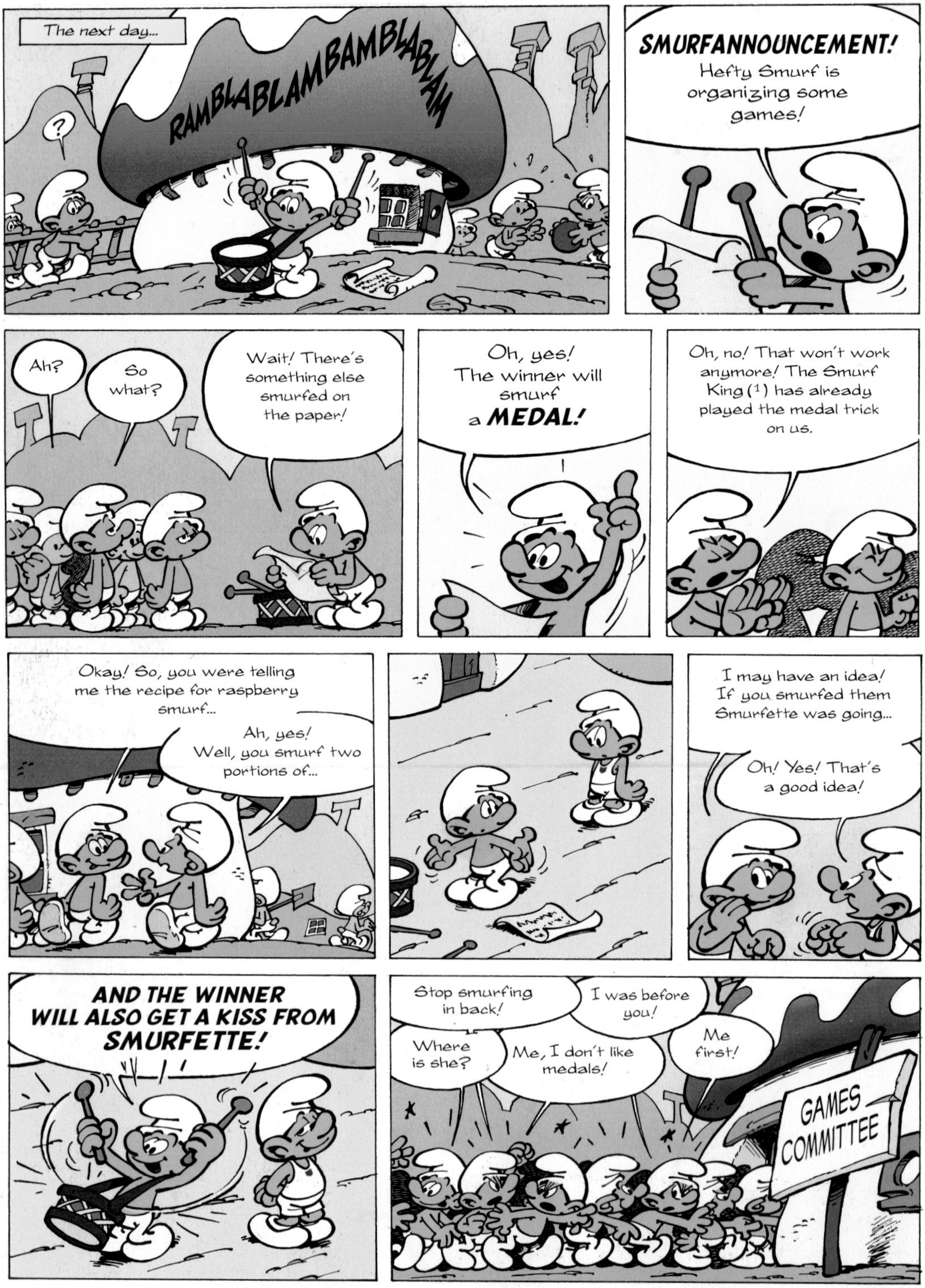

The next day...
RAMBLABLAMBAMBLABLAM
?
SMURFANNOUNCEMENT! Hefty Smurf is organizing some games!
Ah?
So what?
Wait! There's something else smurfed on the paper!
Oh, yes! The winner will smurf a MEDAL!
Oh, no! That won't work anymore! The Smurf King (1) has already played the medal trick on us.
Okay! So, you were telling me the recipe for raspberry smurf...
Ah, yes! Well, you smurf two portions of...
I may have an idea! If you smurfed them Smurfette was going...
Oh! Yes! That's a good idea!
AND THE WINNER WILL ALSO GET A KISS FROM SMURFETTE!
Stop smurfing in back!
I was before you!
Where is she?
Me, I don't like medals!
Me first!
GAMES COMMITTEE

(1) See THE SMURFS #3 "The Smurf King"

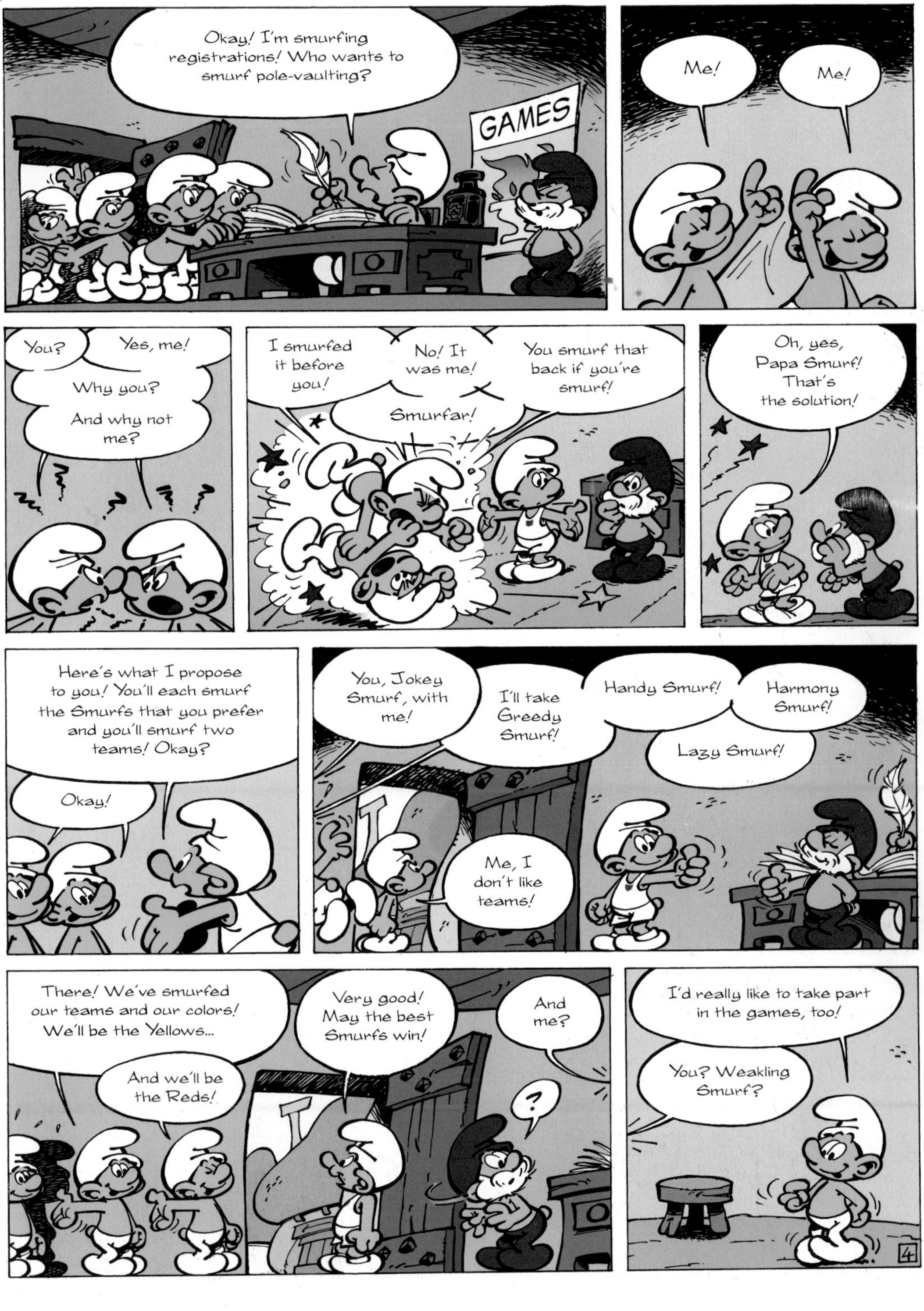
Okay! I'm smurfing registrations! Who wants to smurf pole-vaulting?
GAMES
Me!
Me!
You?
Yes, me!
Why you?
And why not me?
I smurfed it before you!
No! It was me!
You smurf that back if you're smurf!
Smurfar!
Oh, yes, Papa Smurf! That's the solution!
Here's what I propose to you! You'll each smurf the Smurfs that you prefer and you'll smurf two teams! Okay?
Okay!
You, Jokey Smurf, with me!
I'll take Greedy Smurf!
Handy Smurf!
Harmony Smurf!
Lazy Smurf!
Me, I don't like teams!
There! We've smurfed our teams and our colors! We'll be the Yellows...
And we'll be the Reds!
Very good! May the best Smurfs win!
And me?
?
I'd really like to take part in the games, too!
You? Weakling Smurf?
4

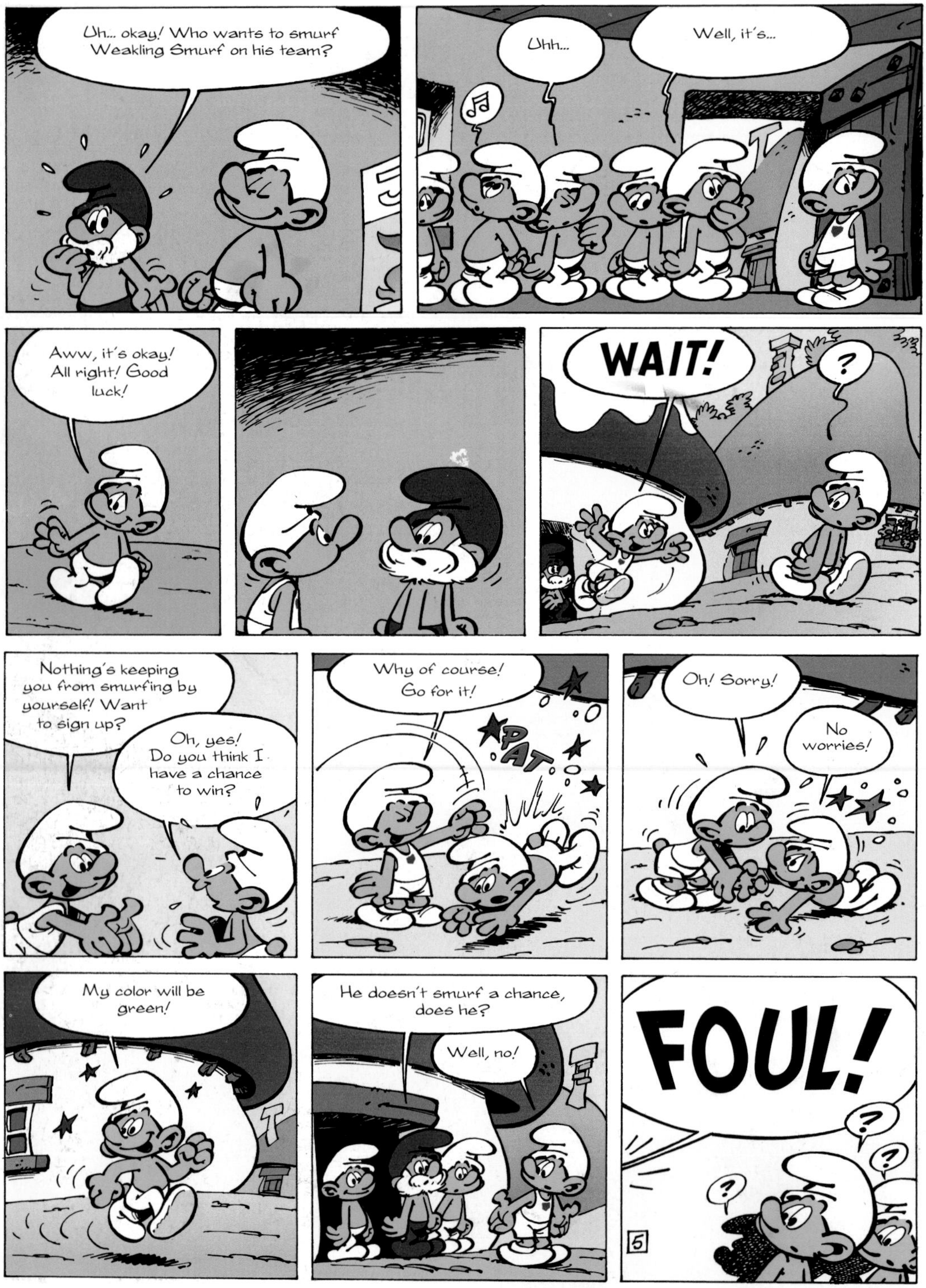

Uh... okay! Who wants to smurf Weakling Smurf on his team?
Uhh...
Well, it's...
Aww, it's okay! All right! Good luck!
WAIT!
?
Nothing's keeping you from smurfing by yourself! Want to sign up?
Oh, yes! Do you think I have a chance to win?
Why of course! Go for it!
PAT
Oh! Sorry!
No worries!
My color will be green!
He doesn't smurf a chance, does he?
Well, no!
FOUL!
?
?
?
5

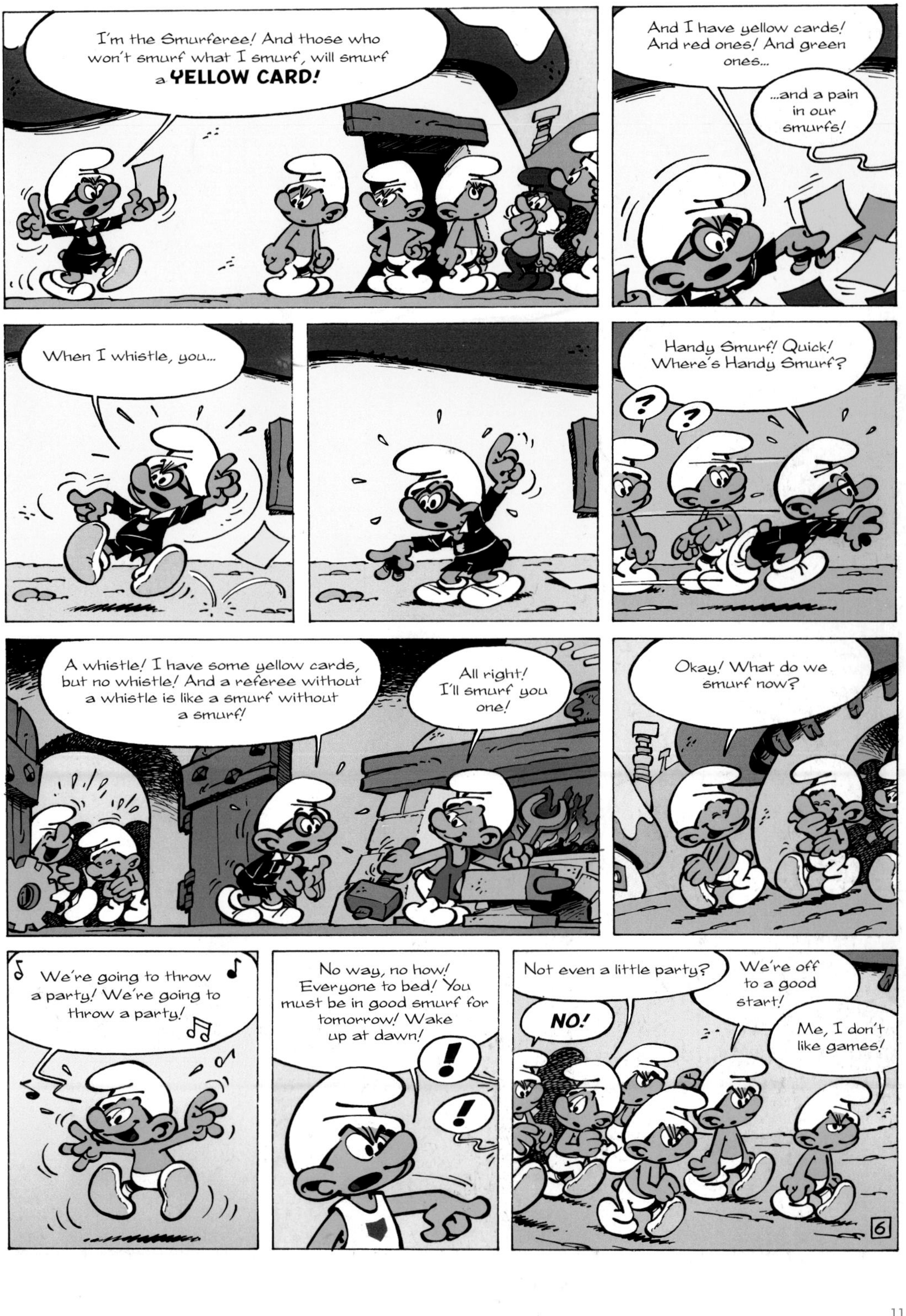
I'm the Smurferee! And those who won't smurf what I smurf, will smurf a YELLOW CARD!
And I have yellow cards! And red ones! And green ones...
...and a pain in our smurfs!
When I whistle, you...
Handy Smurf! Quick! Where's Handy Smurf?
?
?
A whistle! I have some yellow cards, but no whistle! And a referee without a whistle is like a smurf without a smurf!
All right! I'll smurf you one!
Okay! What do we smurf now?
We're going to throw a party! We're going to throw a party!
No way, no how! Everyone to bed! You must be in good smurf for tomorrow! Wake up at dawn!
!
!
Not even a little party?
NO!
We're off to a good start!
Me, I don't like games!
6

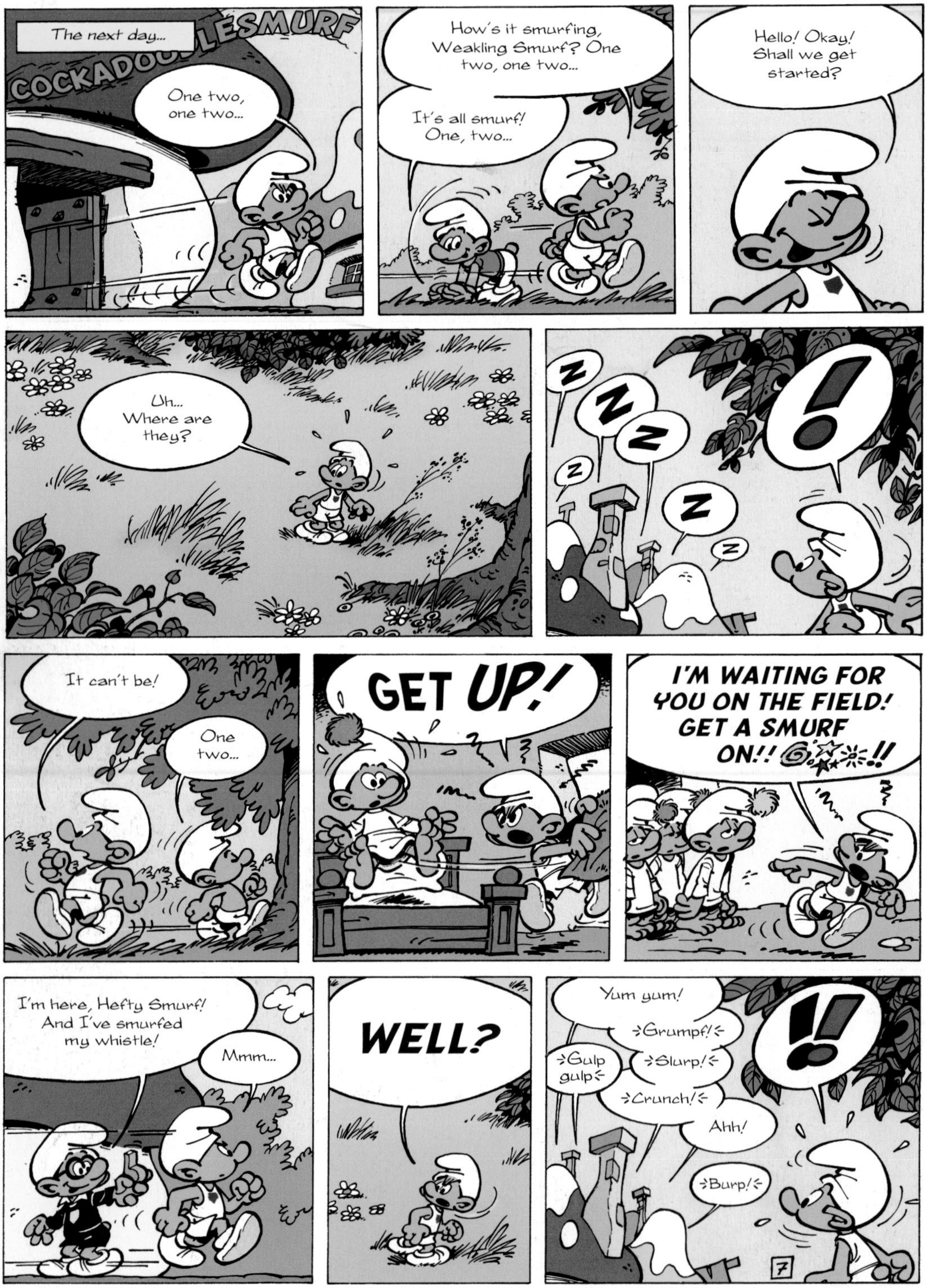

The next day...
COCKADOODLESMURF
One two, one two...
How's it smurfing, Weakling Smurf? One two, one two...
It's all smurf! One, two...
Hello! Okay! Shall we get started?
Uh... Where are they?
Z Z Z Z Z Z Z
!
It can't be!
One two...
GET UP!
I'M WAITING FOR YOU ON THE FIELD! GET A SMURF ON!!
I'm here, Hefty Smurf! And I've smurfed my whistle!
Mmm...
WELL?
Yum yum!
Grumpf!
Gulp gulp
Slurp!
Crunch!
Ahh!
Burp!
!!
7

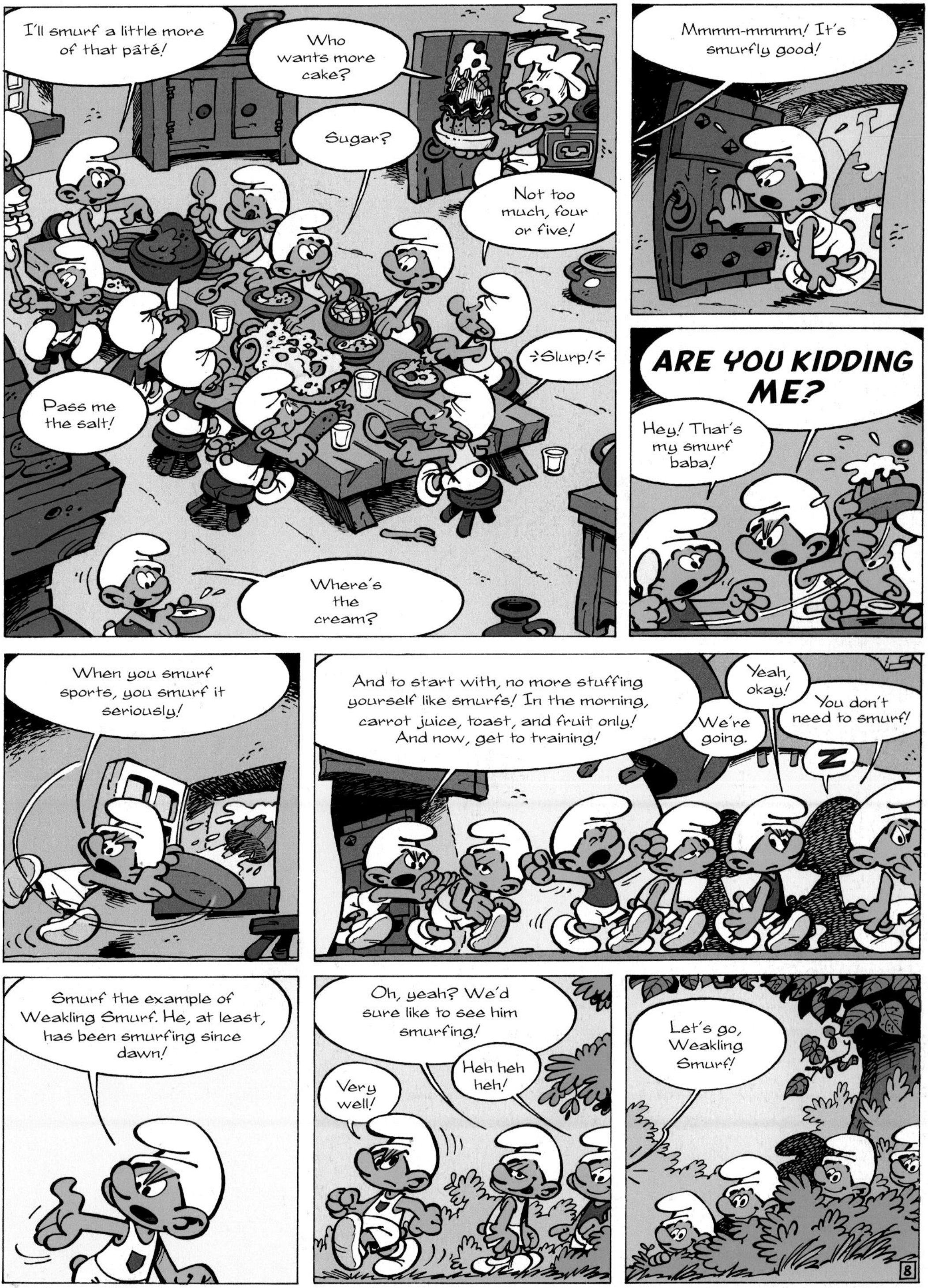
I'll smurf a little more of that pâté!
Who wants more cake?
Sugar?
Not too much, four or five!
Slurp!
Pass me the salt!
Where's the cream?
Mmmm-mmmm! It's smurfly good!
ARE YOU KIDDING ME?
Hey! That's my smurf baba!
When you smurf sports, you smurf it seriously!
And to start with, no more stuffing yourself like smurfs! In the morning, carrot juice, toast, and fruit only! And now, get to training!
We're going.
Yeah, okay!
Z
You don't need to smurf!
Smurf the example of Weakling Smurf. He, at least, has been smurfing since dawn!
Oh, yeah? We'd sure like to see him smurfing!
Very well!
Heh heh heh!
Let's go, Weakling Smurf!
8

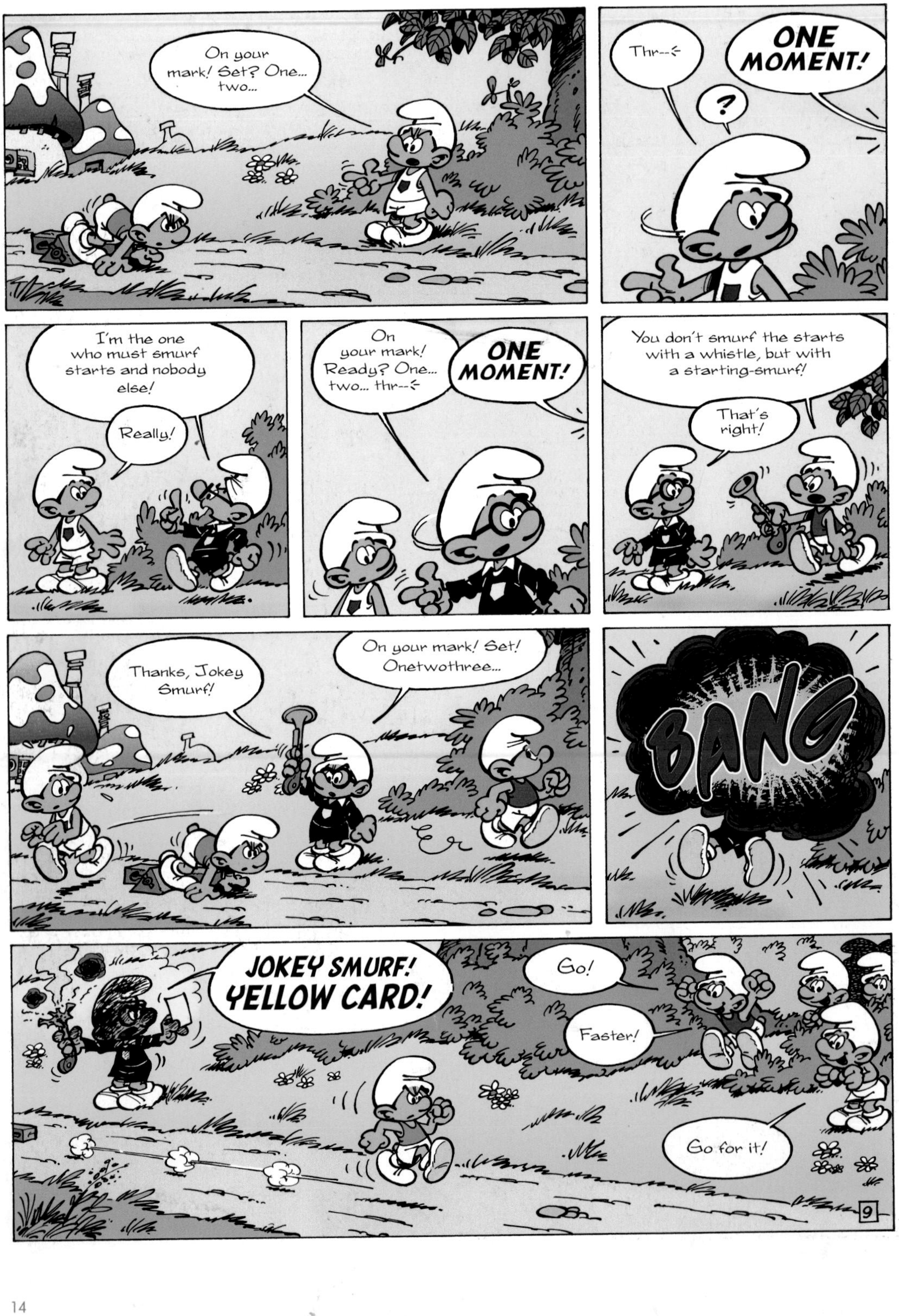

On your mark! Set? One... two...
Thr--
?
ONE MOMENT!
I'm the one who must smurf starts and nobody else!
Really!
On your mark! Ready? One... two... thr--
ONE MOMENT!
You don't smurf the starts with a whistle, but with a starting-smurf!
That's right!
Thanks, Jokey Smurf!
On your mark! Set! Onetwothree...
BANG
JOKEY SMURF! YELLOW CARD!
Go!
Faster!
Go for it!
9

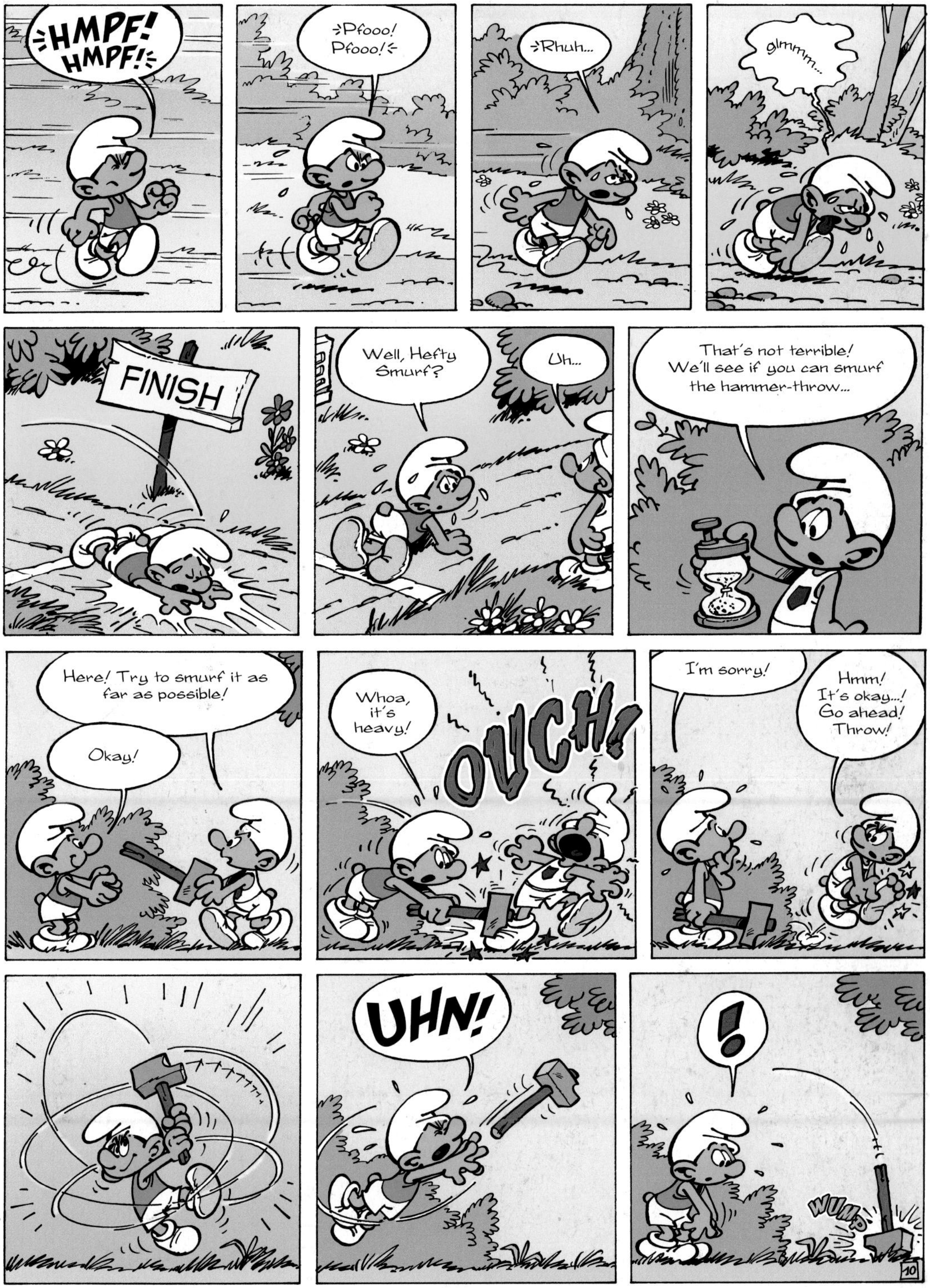
HMPF! HMPF!
Pfooo! Pfooo!
Rhuh...
glmmm...
FINISH
Well, Hefty Smurf?
Uh...
That's not terrible! We'll see if you can smurf the hammer-throw...
Here! Try to smurf it as far as possible!
Okay!
Whoa, it's heavy!
OUCH!
I'm sorry!
Hmm! It's okay...! Go ahead! Throw!
UHN!
!
WUMP
10

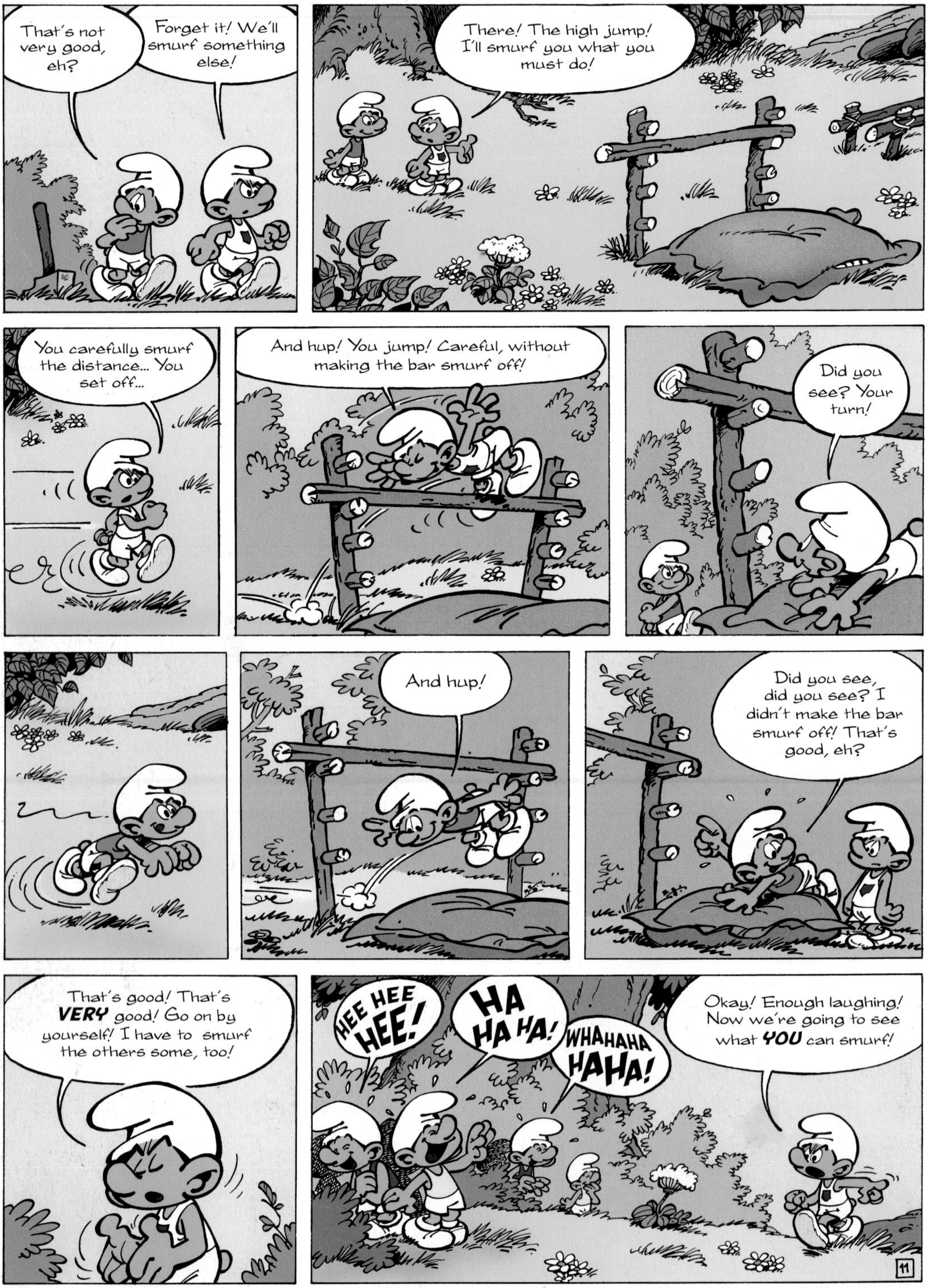

That's not very good, eh?
Forget it! We'll smurf something else!
There! The high jump! I'll smurf you what you must do!
You carefully smurf the distance... You set off...
And hup! You jump! Careful, without making the bar smurf off!
Did you see? Your turn!
And hup!
Did you see, did you see? I didn't make the bar smurf off! That's good, eh?
That's good! That's VERY good! Go on by yourself! I have to smurf the others some, too!
HEE HEE HEE!
HA HA HA!
WHAHAHA HAHA!
Okay! Enough laughing! Now we're going to see what YOU can smurf!
11

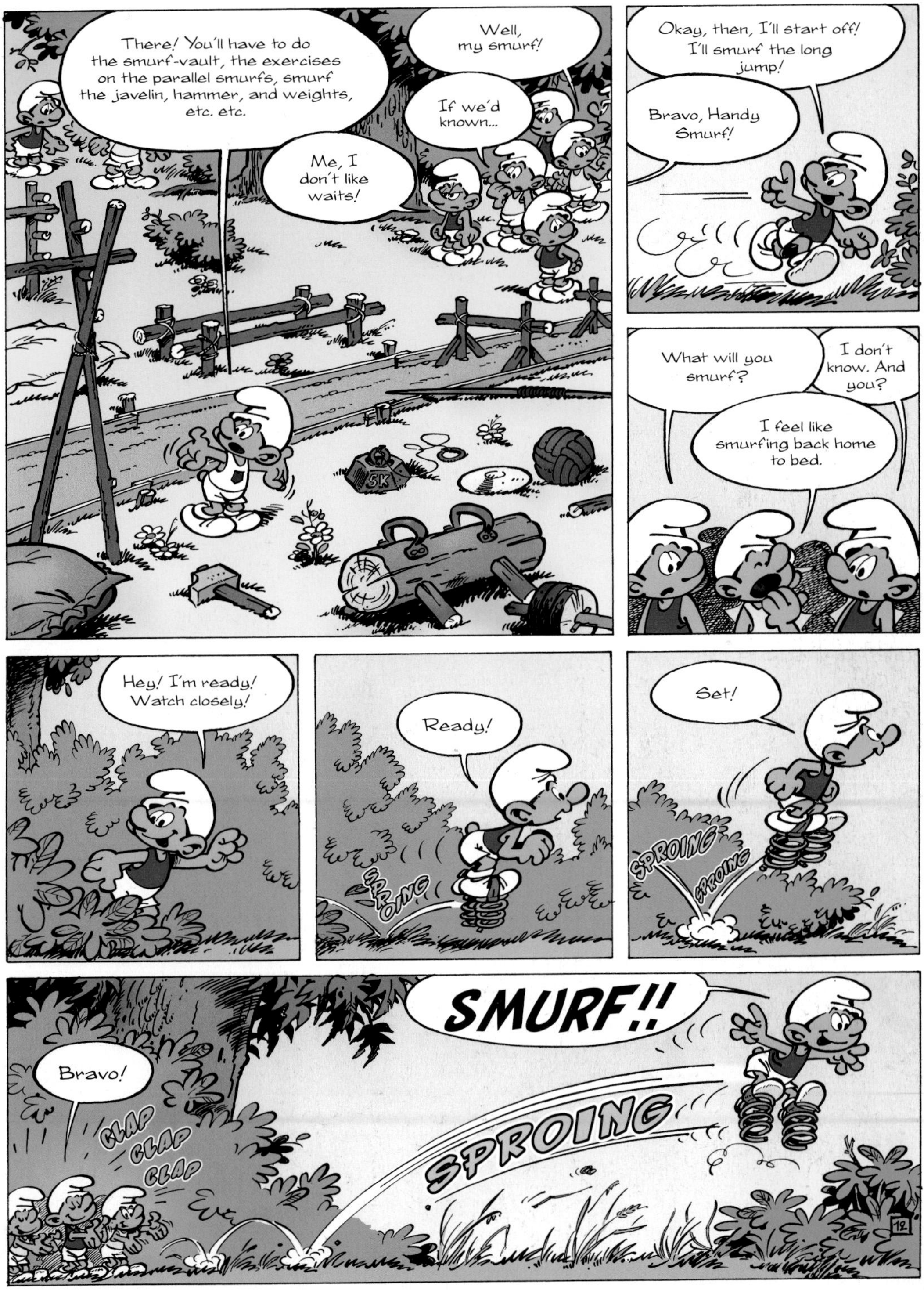
There! You'll have to do the smurf-vault, the exercises on the parallel smurfs, smurf the javelin, hammer, and weights, etc. etc.
Me, I don't like waits!
If we'd known...
Well, my smurf!
5K
Okay, then, I'll start off! I'll smurf the long jump!
Bravo, Handy Smurf!
What will you smurf?
I don't know. And you?
I feel like smurfing back home to bed.
Hey! I'm ready! Watch closely!
Ready!
SPROING
Set!
SPROING
SPROING
SMURF!!
SPROING
Bravo!
CLAP
CLAP
CLAP
12

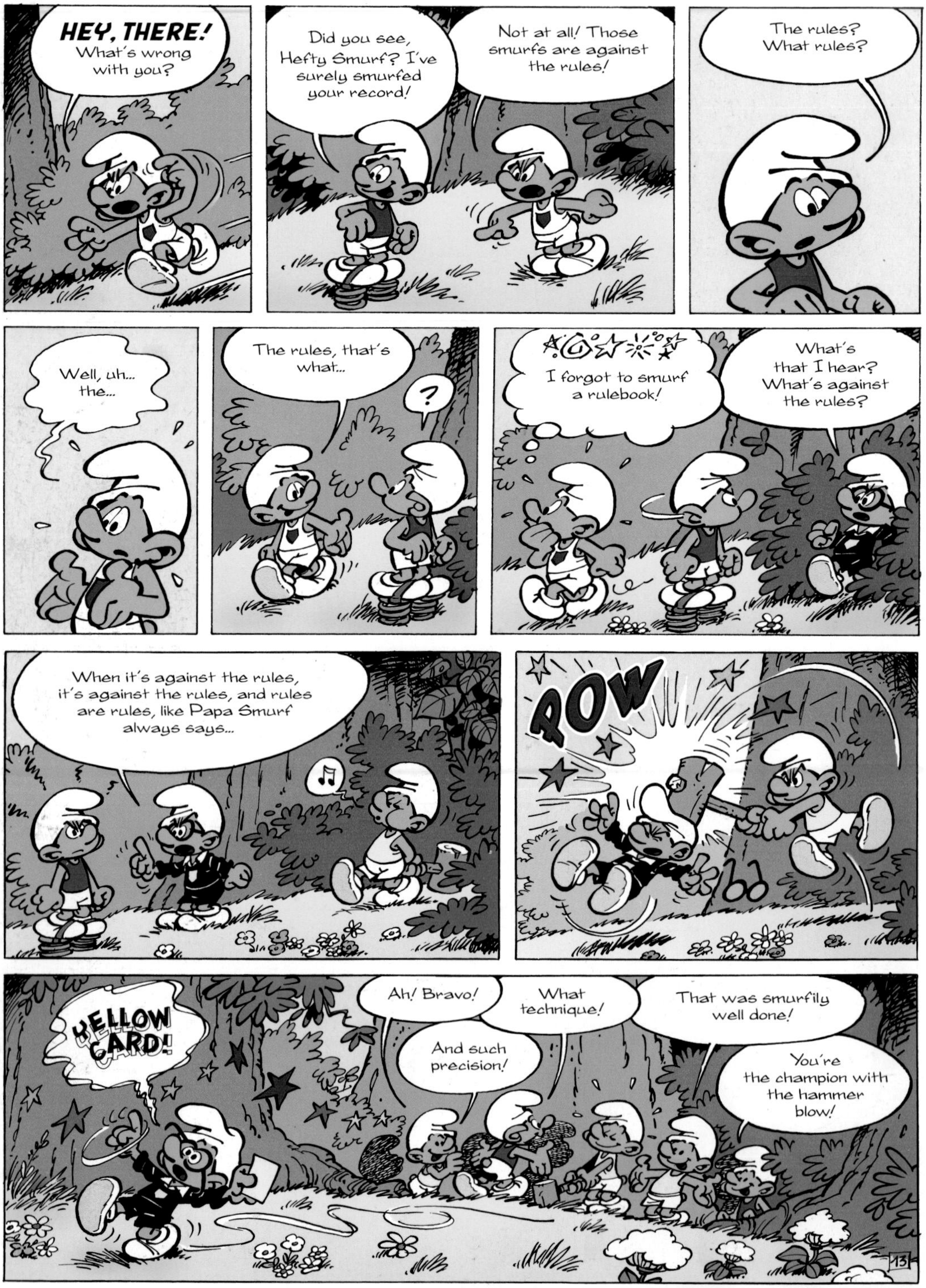
HEY, THERE! What's wrong with you?
Did you see, Hefty Smurf? I've surely smurfed your record!
Not at all! Those smurfs are against the rules!
The rules? What rules?
Well, uh... the...
The rules, that's what...
?
I forgot to smurf a rulebook!
What's that I hear? What's against the rules?
When it's against the rules, it's against the rules, and rules are rules, like Papa Smurf always says...
POW
YELLOW CARD!
Ah! Bravo!
What technique!
And such precision!
That was smurfily well done!
You're the champion with the hammer blow!
13

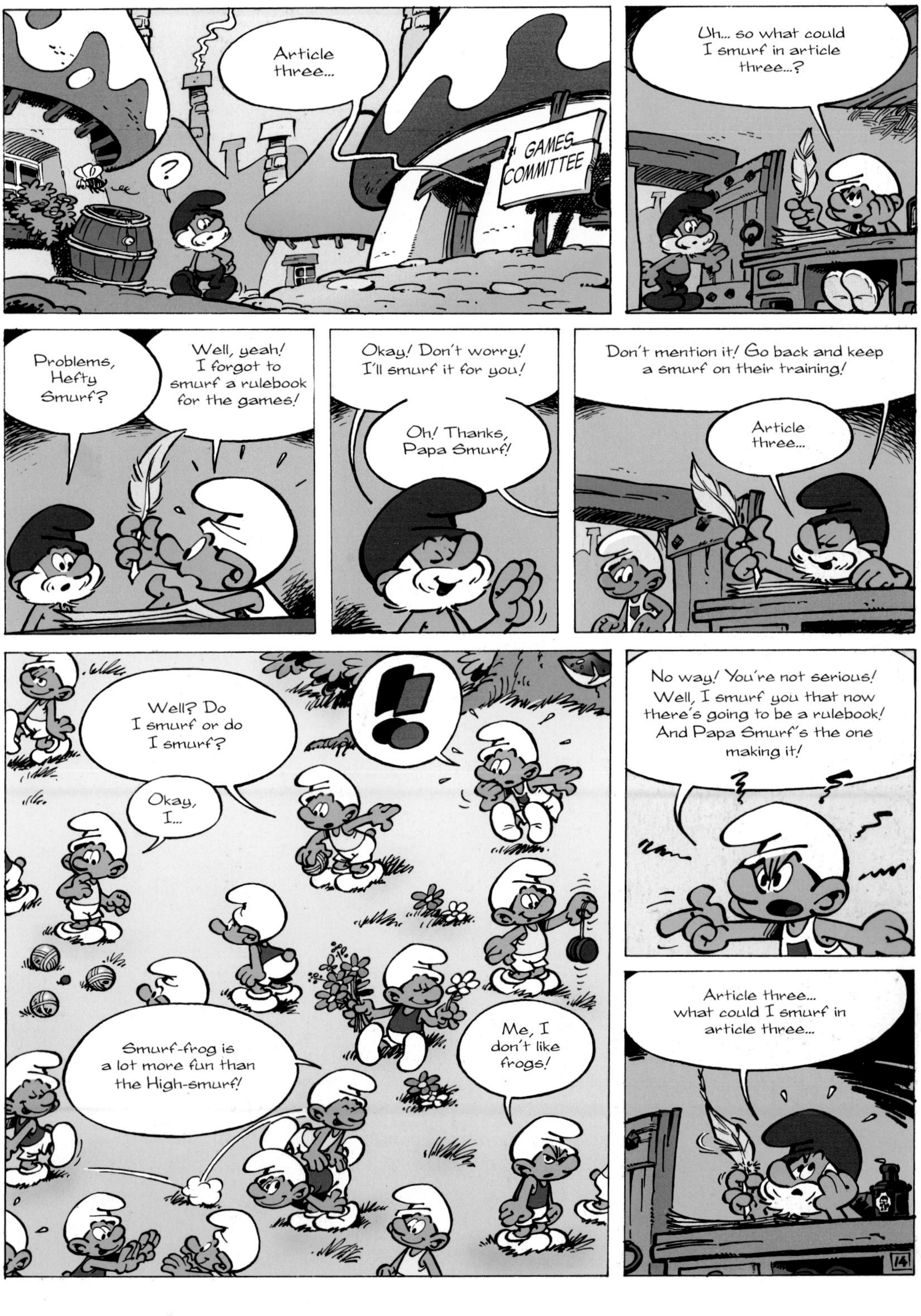
Article three...
Uh... so what could I smurf in article three...?
Problems, Hefty Smurf?
Well, yeah! I forgot to smurf a rulebook for the games!
Okay! Don't worry! I'll smurf it for you!
Oh! Thanks, Papa Smurf!
Don't mention it! Go back and keep a smurf on their training!
Article three...
Well? Do I smurf or do I smurf?
Okay, I...
Smurf-frog is a lot more fun than the High-smurf!
Me, I don't like frogs!
No way! You're not serious! Well, I smurf you that now there's going to be a rulebook! And Papa Smurf's the one making it!
Article three... what could I smurf in article three...
GAMES COMMITTEE
14

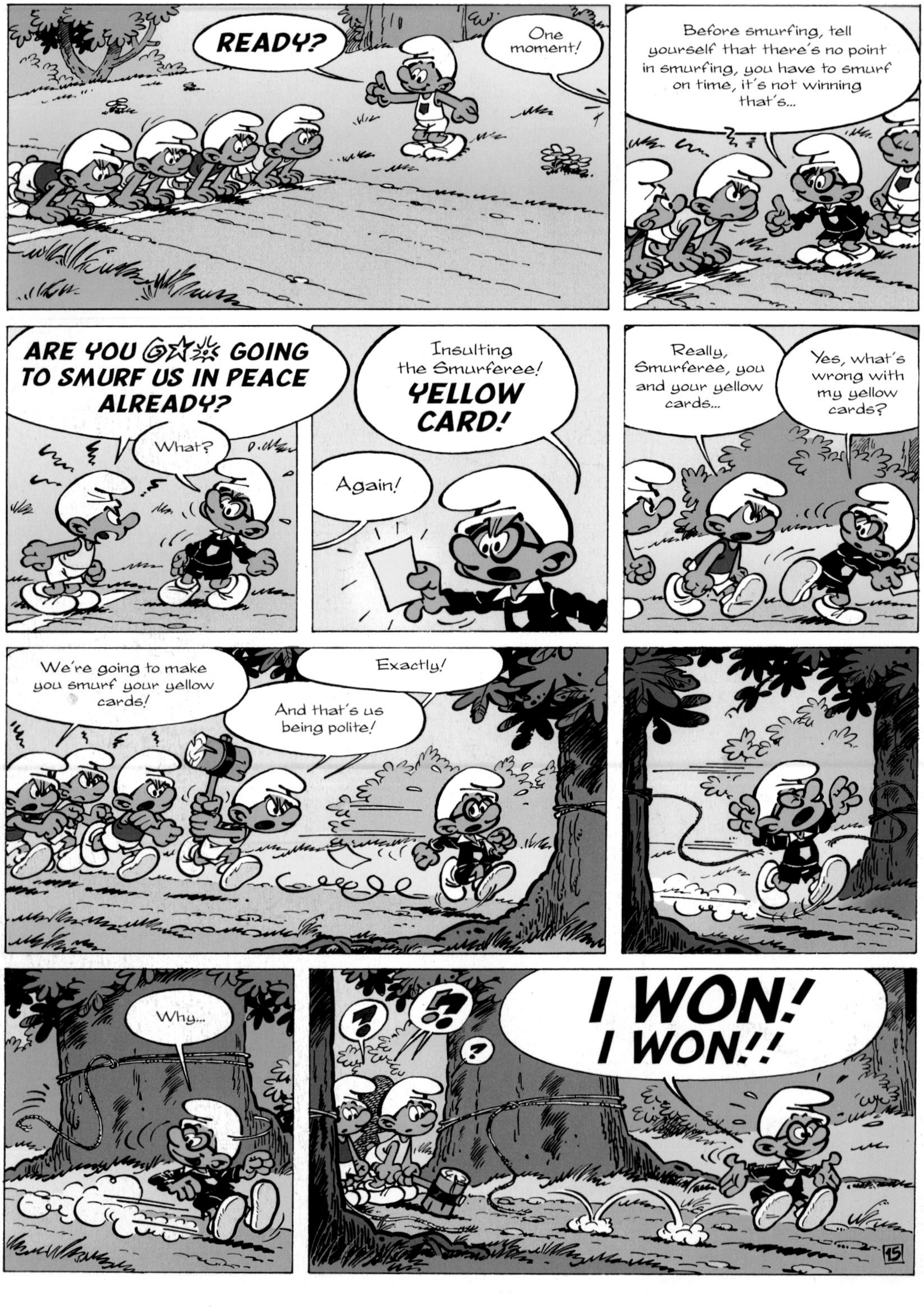

READY?
One moment!
Before smurfing, tell yourself that there's no point in smurfing, you have to smurf on time, it's not winning that's...
ARE YOU @☆✹ GOING TO SMURF US IN PEACE ALREADY?
What?
Insulting the Smurferee! YELLOW CARD!
Again!
Really, Smurferee, you and your yellow cards...
Yes, what's wrong with my yellow cards?
We're going to make you smurf your yellow cards!
Exactly!
And that's us being polite!
Why...
?
?!
?
I WON! I WON!!
15

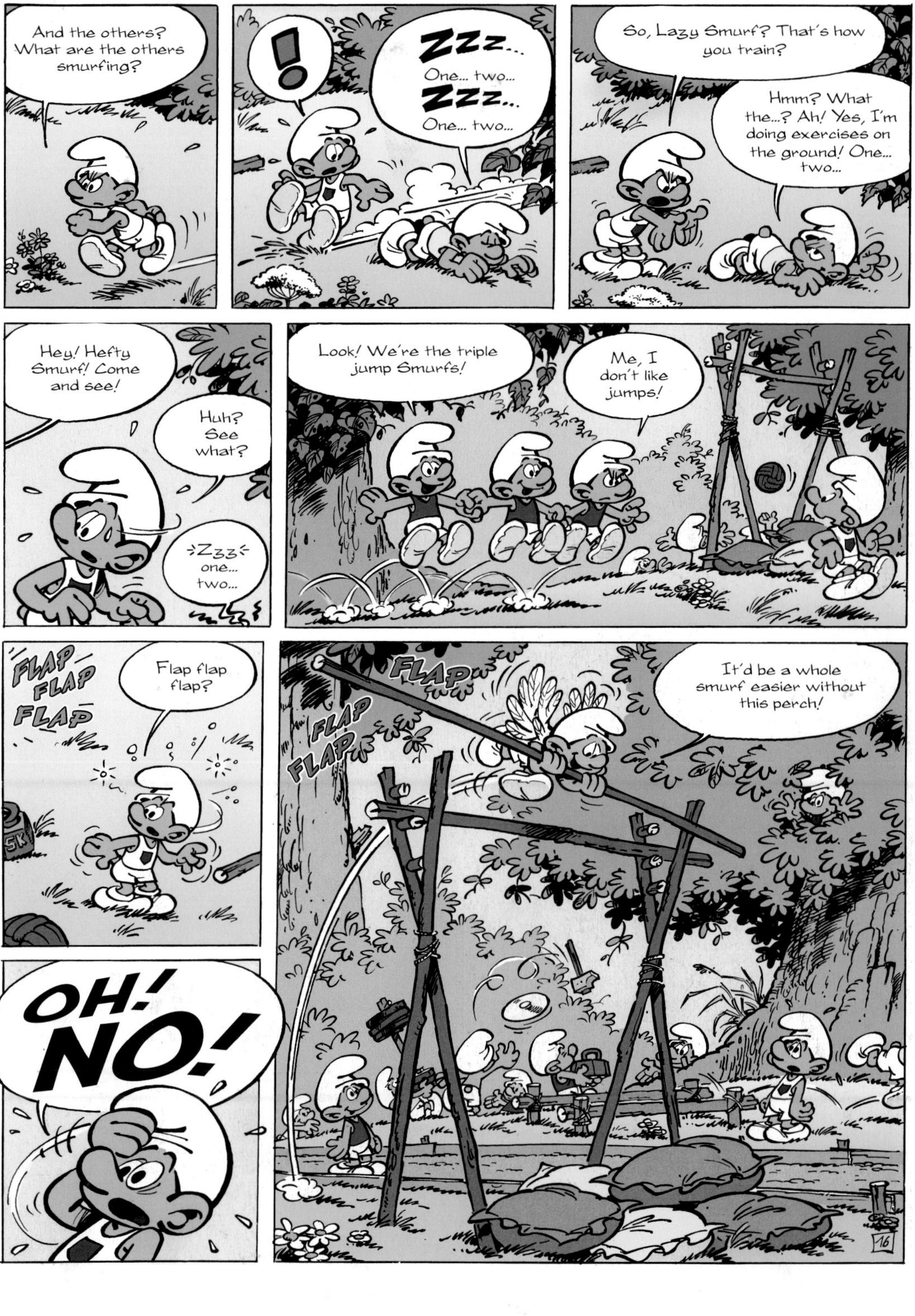
And the others? What are the others smurfing?
!
Zzz... One... two... Zzz... One... two...
So, Lazy Smurf? That's how you train?
Hmm? What the...? Ah! Yes, I'm doing exercises on the ground! One... two...
Hey! Hefty Smurf! Come and see!
Huh? See what?
Zzz one... two...
Look! We're the triple jump Smurfs!
Me, I don't like jumps!
FLAP FLAP FLAP
Flap flap flap?
FLAP
FLAP FLAP
It'd be a whole smurf easier without this perch!
OH! NO!
16

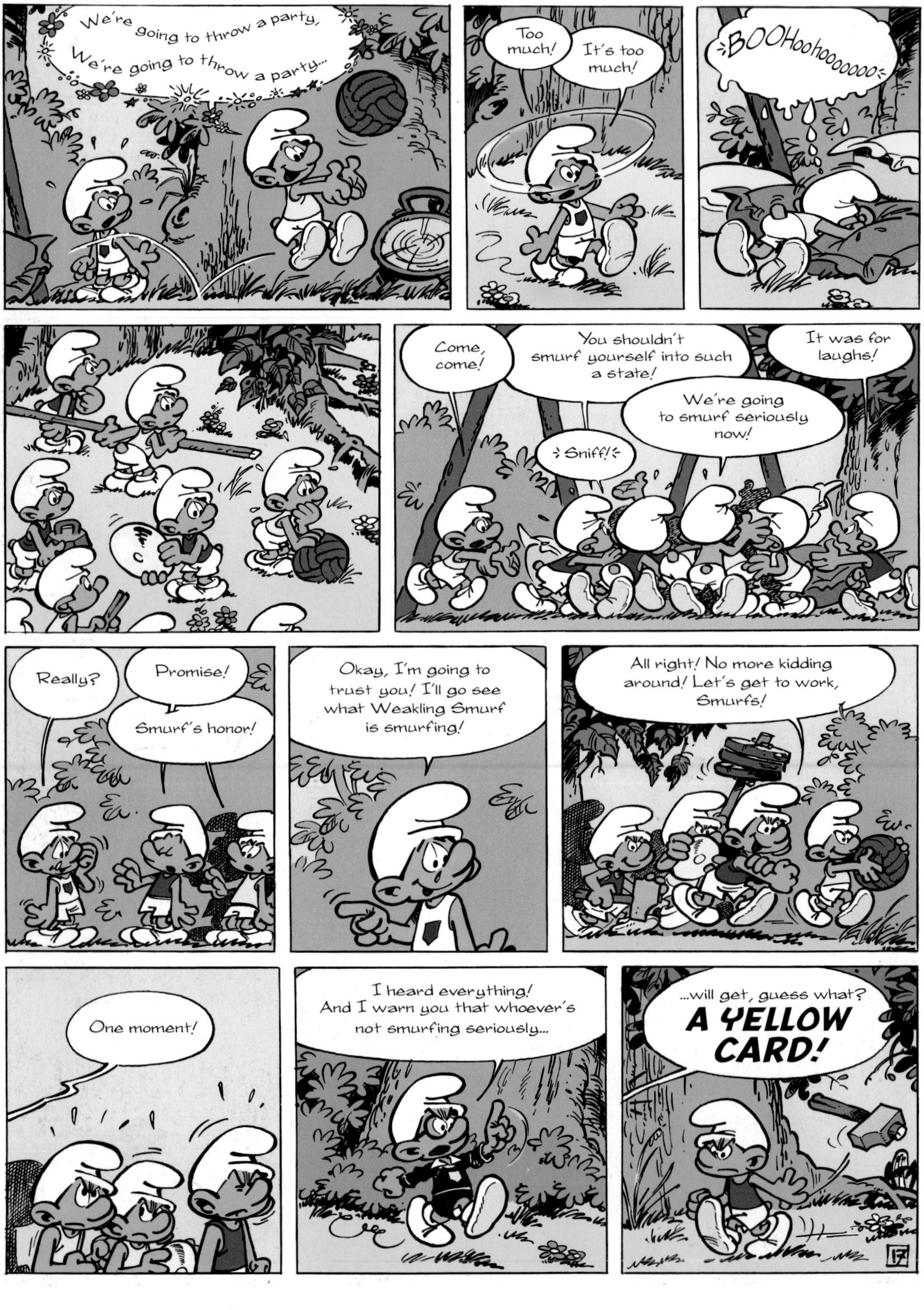
We're going to throw a party,
We're going to throw a party...
Too much!
It's too much!
BOOHoohoooooo
Come, come!
You shouldn't smurf yourself into such a state!
It was for laughs!
We're going to smurf seriously now!
Sniff!
Really?
Promise!
Smurf's honor!
Okay, I'm going to trust you! I'll go see what Weakling Smurf is smurfing!
All right! No more kidding around! Let's get to work, Smurfs!
One moment!
I heard everything! And I warn you that whoever's not smurfing seriously...
...will get, guess what?
A YELLOW CARD!
17

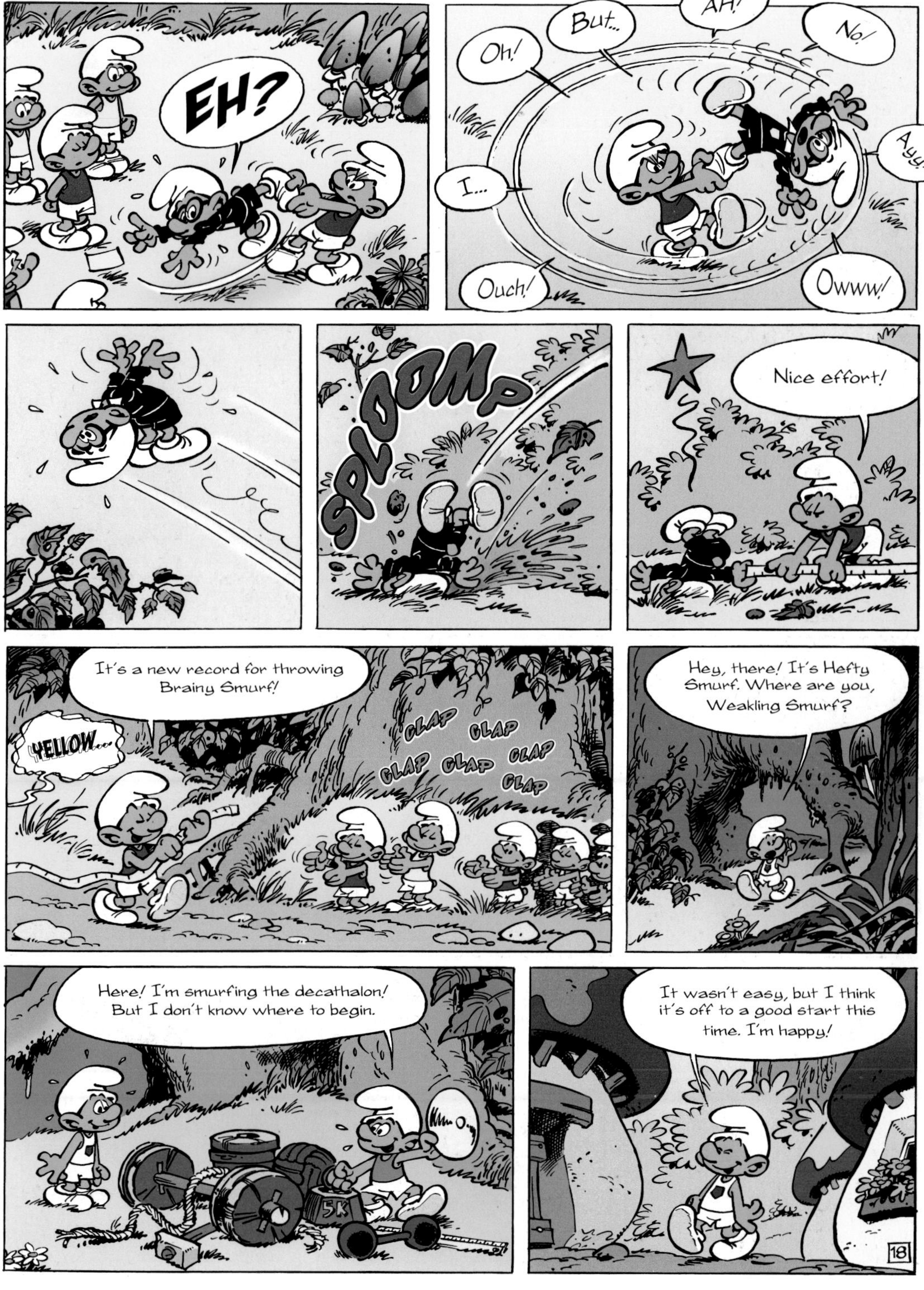

EH?
Oh!
But...
AH!
No!
Ayy!
I...
Ouch!
Owww!
SPLOOMP
Nice effort!
It's a new record for throwing Brainy Smurf!
YELLOW...
CLAP CLAP CLAP CLAP CLAP CLAP
Hey, there! It's Hefty Smurf. Where are you, Weakling Smurf?
Here! I'm smurfing the decathalon! But I don't know where to begin.
5K
It wasn't easy, but I think it's off to a good start this time. I'm happy!
18

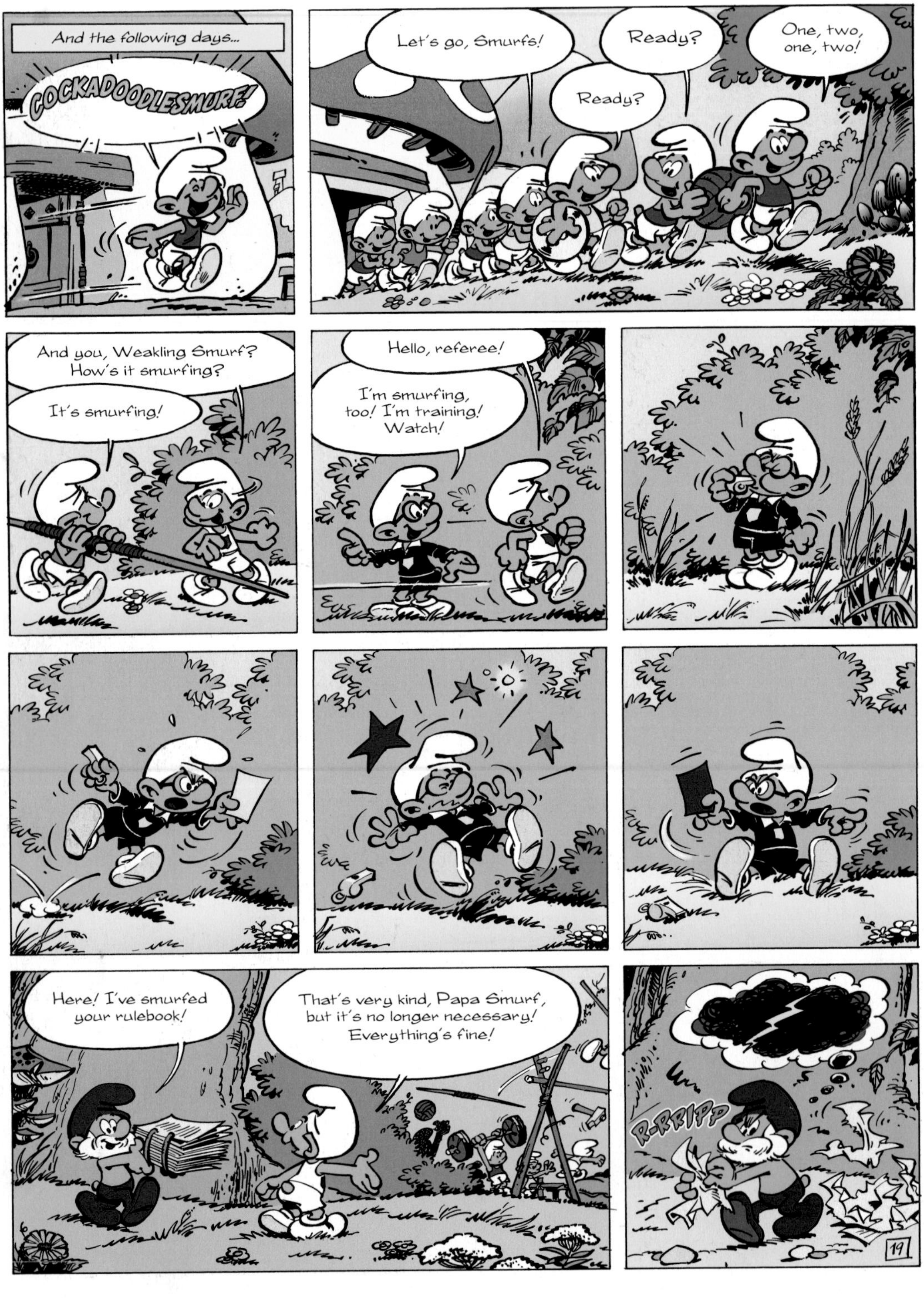

And the following days...
COCKADOODLESMURF!
Let's go, Smurfs!
Ready?
Ready?
One, two, one, two!
And you, Weakling Smurf? How's it smurfing?
It's smurfing!
Hello, referee!
I'm smurfing, too! I'm training! Watch!
Here! I've smurfed your rulebook!
That's very kind, Papa Smurf, but it's no longer necessary! Everything's fine!
R-RRIPP
19

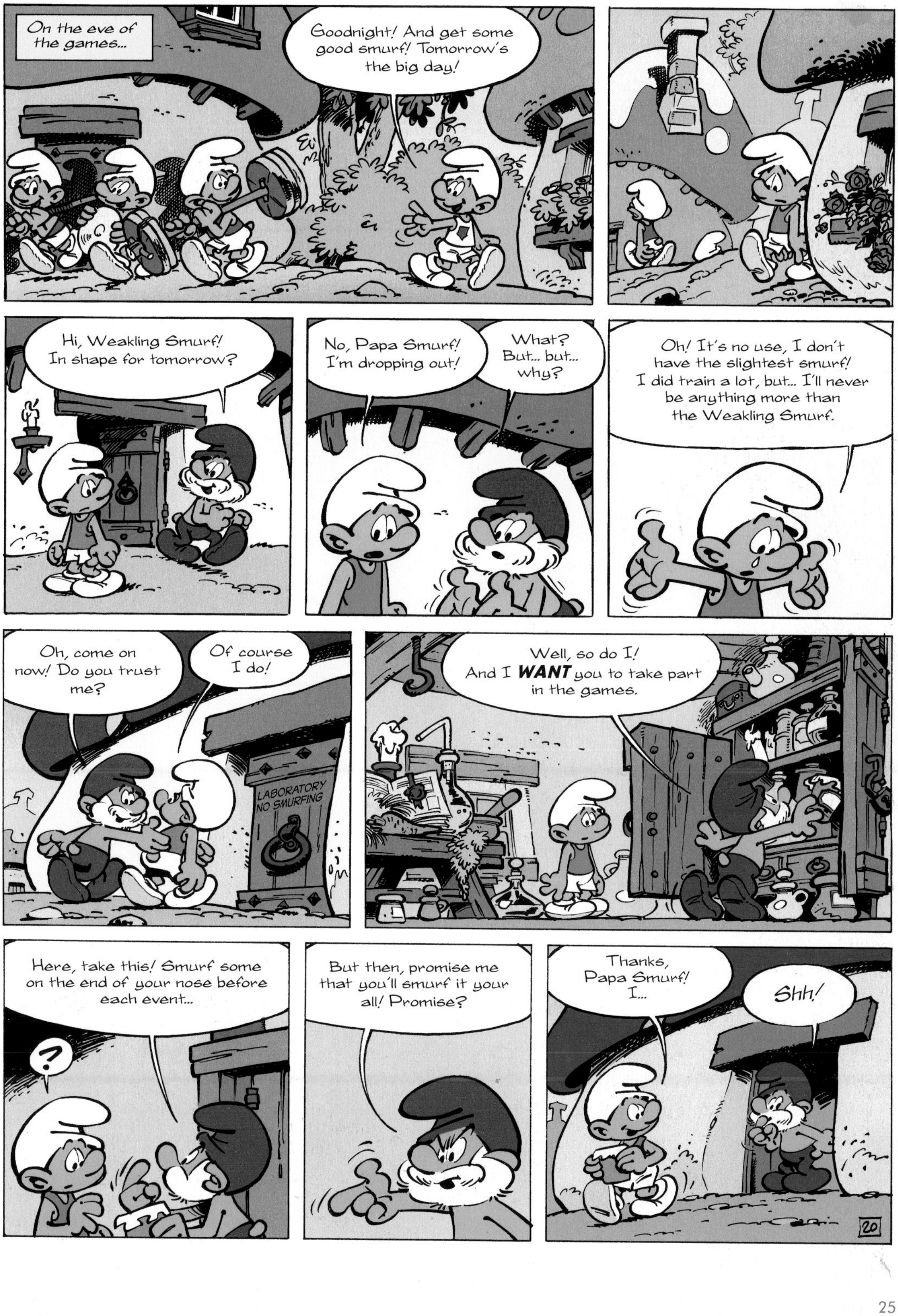
On the eve of the games...
Goodnight! And get some good smurf! Tomorrow's the big day!
Hi, Weakling Smurf! In shape for tomorrow?
No, Papa Smurf! I'm dropping out!
What? But... but... why?
Oh! It's no use, I don't have the slightest smurf! I did train a lot, but... I'll never be anything more than the Weakling Smurf.
Oh, come on now! Do you trust me?
Of course I do!
LABORATORY NO SMURFING
Well, so do I! And I **WANT** you to take part in the games.
Here, take this! Smurf some on the end of your nose before each event...
?
But then, promise me that you'll smurf it your all! Promise?
Thanks, Papa Smurf! I...
Shh!
20

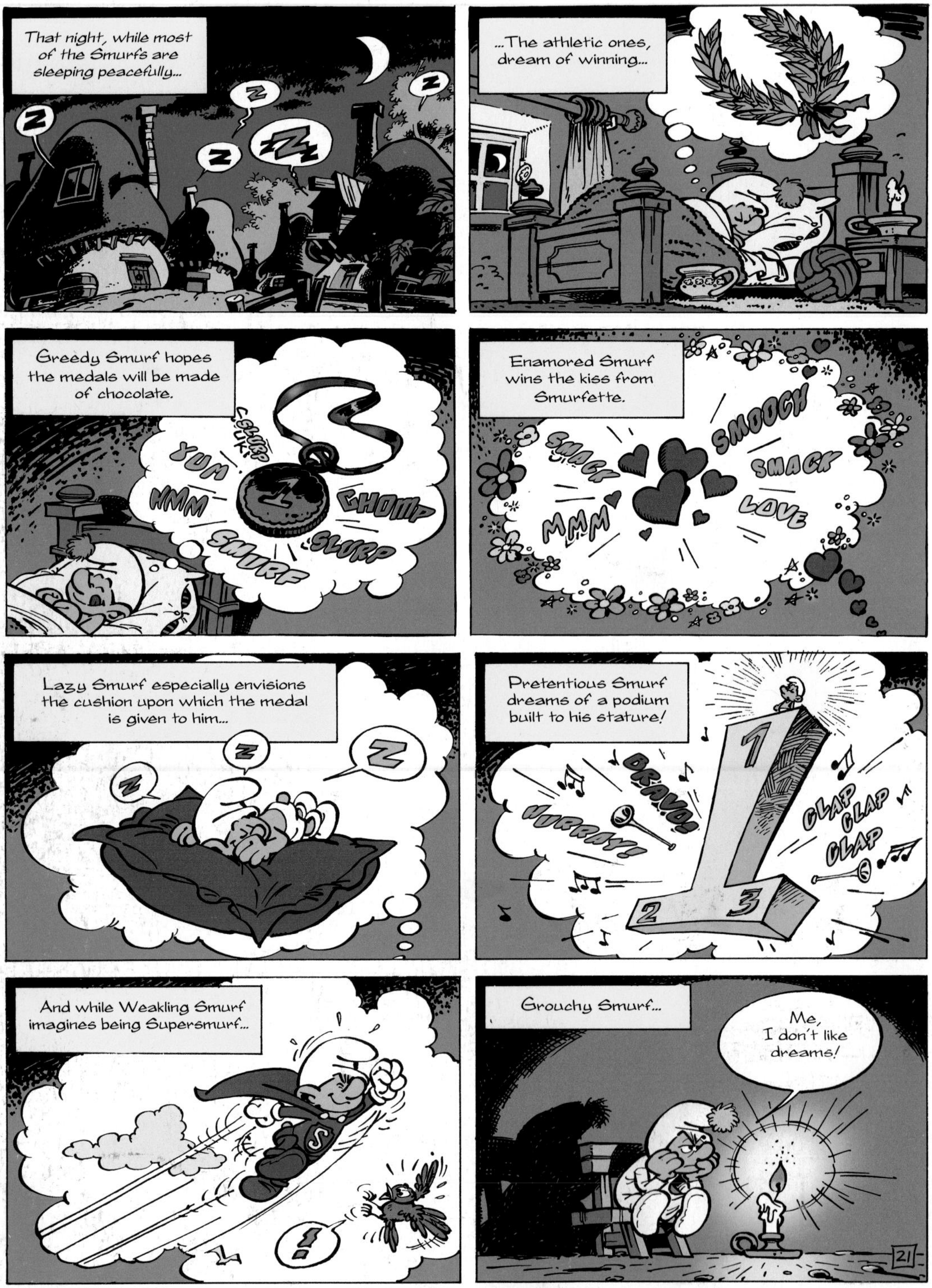

That night, while most of the Smurfs are sleeping peacefully...
Z
Z
Z
ZZ
Z
...The athletic ones, dream of winning...
Greedy Smurf hopes the medals will be made of chocolate.
YUM
HMM
SMURF
SLURP
CHOMP
Enamored Smurf wins the kiss from Smurfette.
SMACK
MMM
SMOOCH
SMACK
LOVE
Lazy Smurf especially envisions the cushion upon which the medal is given to him...
Z
Z
Z
Pretentious Smurf dreams of a podium built to his stature!
BRAVO!
HURRAY!
CLAP
CLAP
CLAP
1
2
3
And while Weakling Smurf imagines being Supersmurf...
S
!
Grouchy Smurf...
Me, I don't like dreams!
21

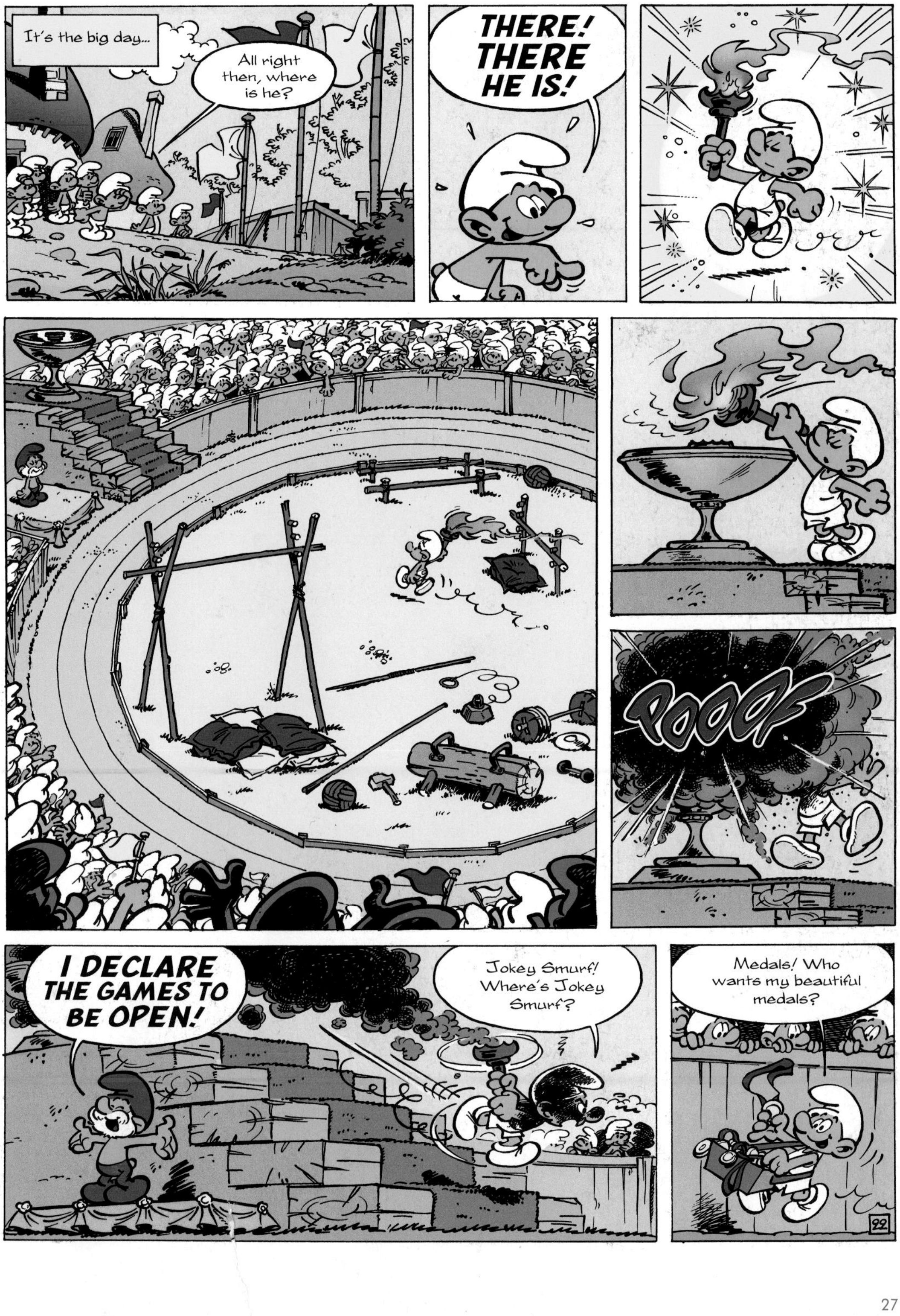

It's the big day...
All right then, where is he?
THERE! THERE HE IS!
POOOF
I DECLARE THE GAMES TO BE OPEN!
Jokey Smurf! Where's Jokey Smurf?
Medals! Who wants my beautiful medals?
22

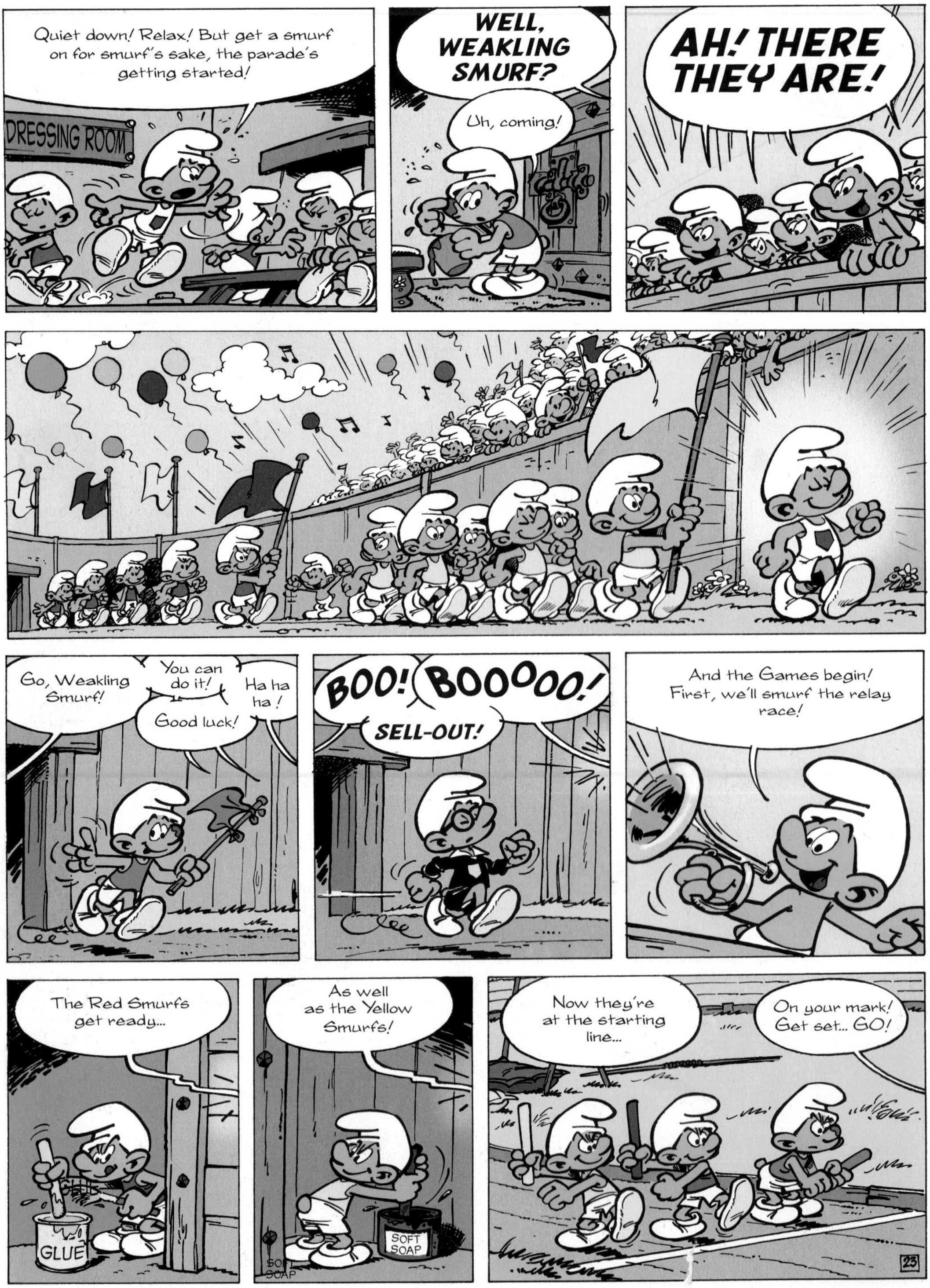

Quiet down! Relax! But get a smurf on for smurf's sake, the parade's getting started!
DRESSING ROOM
WELL, WEAKLING SMURF?
Uh, coming!
AH! THERE THEY ARE!
Go, Weakling Smurf!
You can do it!
Good luck!
Ha ha ha!
BOO! BOOOOO!
SELL-OUT!
And the Games begin! First, we'll smurf the relay race!
The Red Smurfs get ready...
GLUE
As well as the Yellow Smurfs!
SOFT SOAP
SOFT SOAP
Now they're at the starting line...
On your mark! Get set... GO!
23

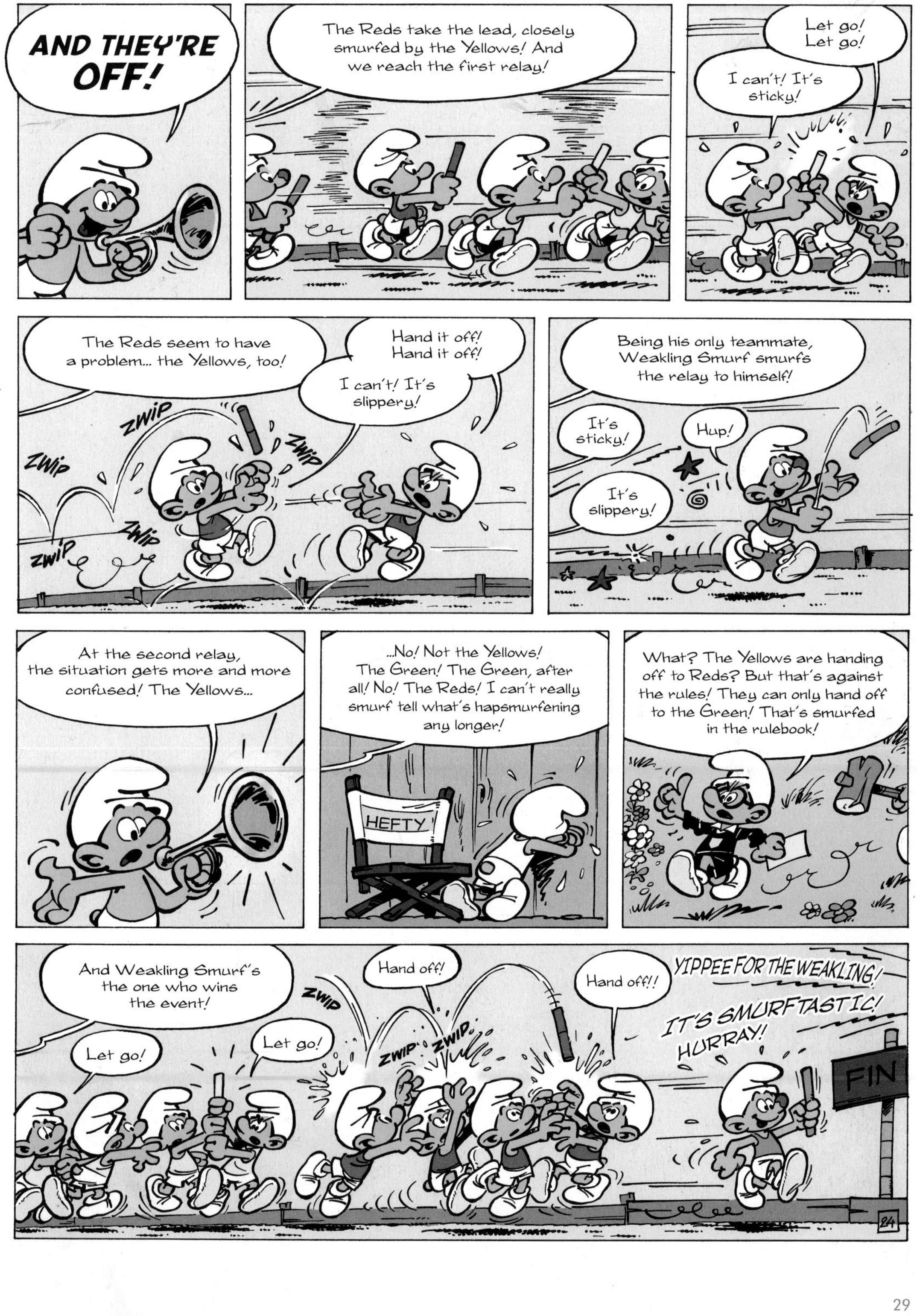
AND THEY'RE OFF!
The Reds take the lead, closely smurfed by the Yellows! And we reach the first relay!
Let go! Let go!
I can't! It's sticky!
The Reds seem to have a problem... the Yellows, too!
Hand it off! Hand it off!
I can't! It's slippery!
ZWIP
ZWIP
ZWIP
ZWIP
ZWIP
Being his only teammate, Weakling Smurf smurfs the relay to himself!
It's sticky!
Hup!
It's slippery!
At the second relay, the situation gets more and more confused! The Yellows...
...No! Not the Yellows! The Green! The Green, after all! No! The Reds! I can't really smurf tell what's hapsmurfening any longer!
HEFTY
What? The Yellows are handing off to Reds? But that's against the rules! They can only hand off to the Green! That's smurfed in the rulebook!
And Weakling Smurf's the one who wins the event!
Hand off!
Hand off!!
YIPPEE FOR THE WEAKLING!
IT'S SMURFTASTIC! HURRAY!
ZWIP
Let go!
Let go!
ZWIP
ZWIP
FIN
24

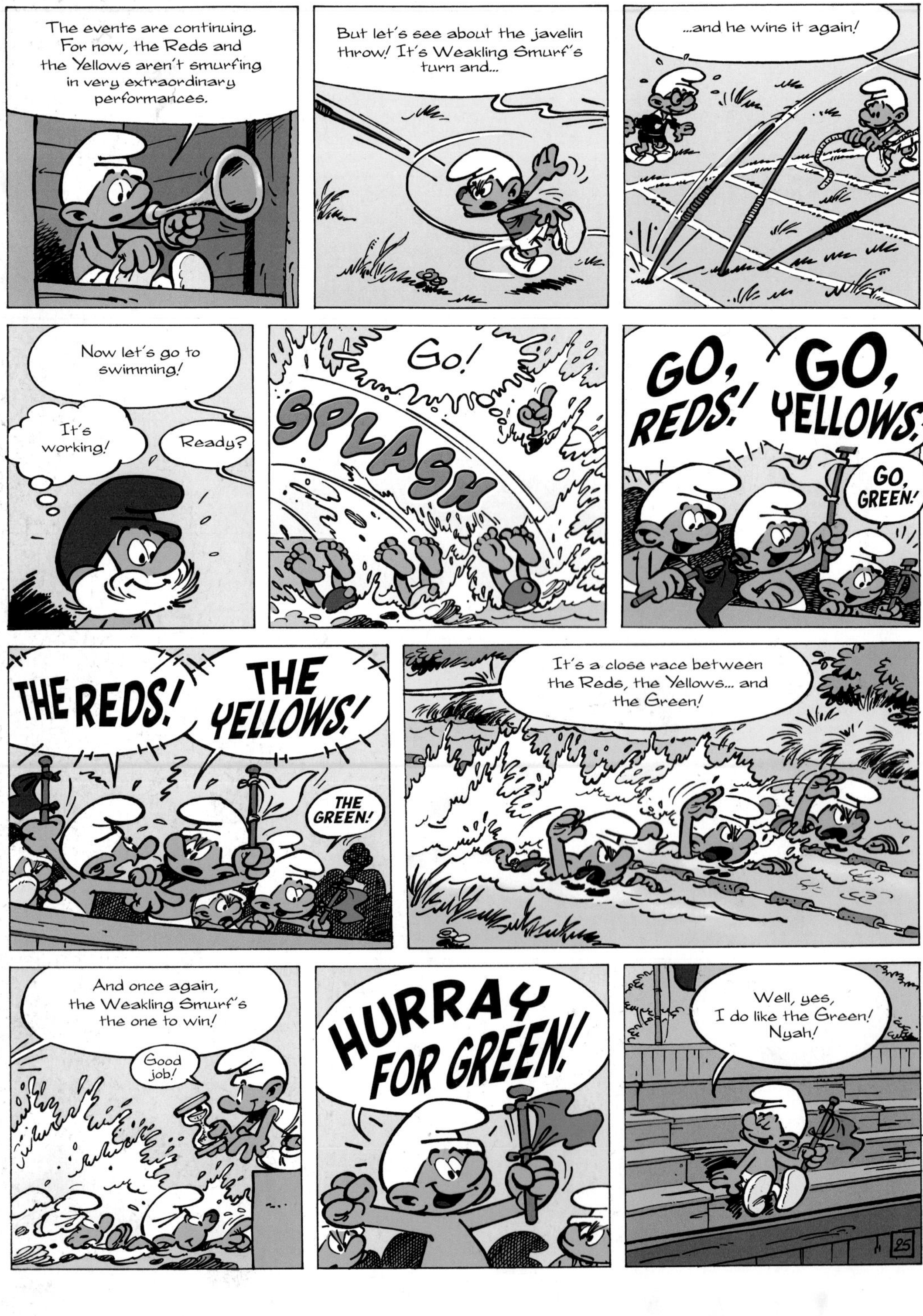

The events are continuing. For now, the Reds and the Yellows aren't smurfing in very extraordinary performances.
But let's see about the javelin throw! It's Weakling Smurf's turn and...
...and he wins it again!
Now let's go to swimming!
It's working!
Ready?
Go!
SPLASH
GO, REDS!
GO, YELLOWS!
GO, GREEN!
THE REDS!
THE YELLOWS!
THE GREEN!
It's a close race between the Reds, the Yellows... and the Green!
And once again, the Weakling Smurf's the one to win!
Good job!
HURRAY FOR GREEN!
Well, yes, I do like the Green! Nyah!
25

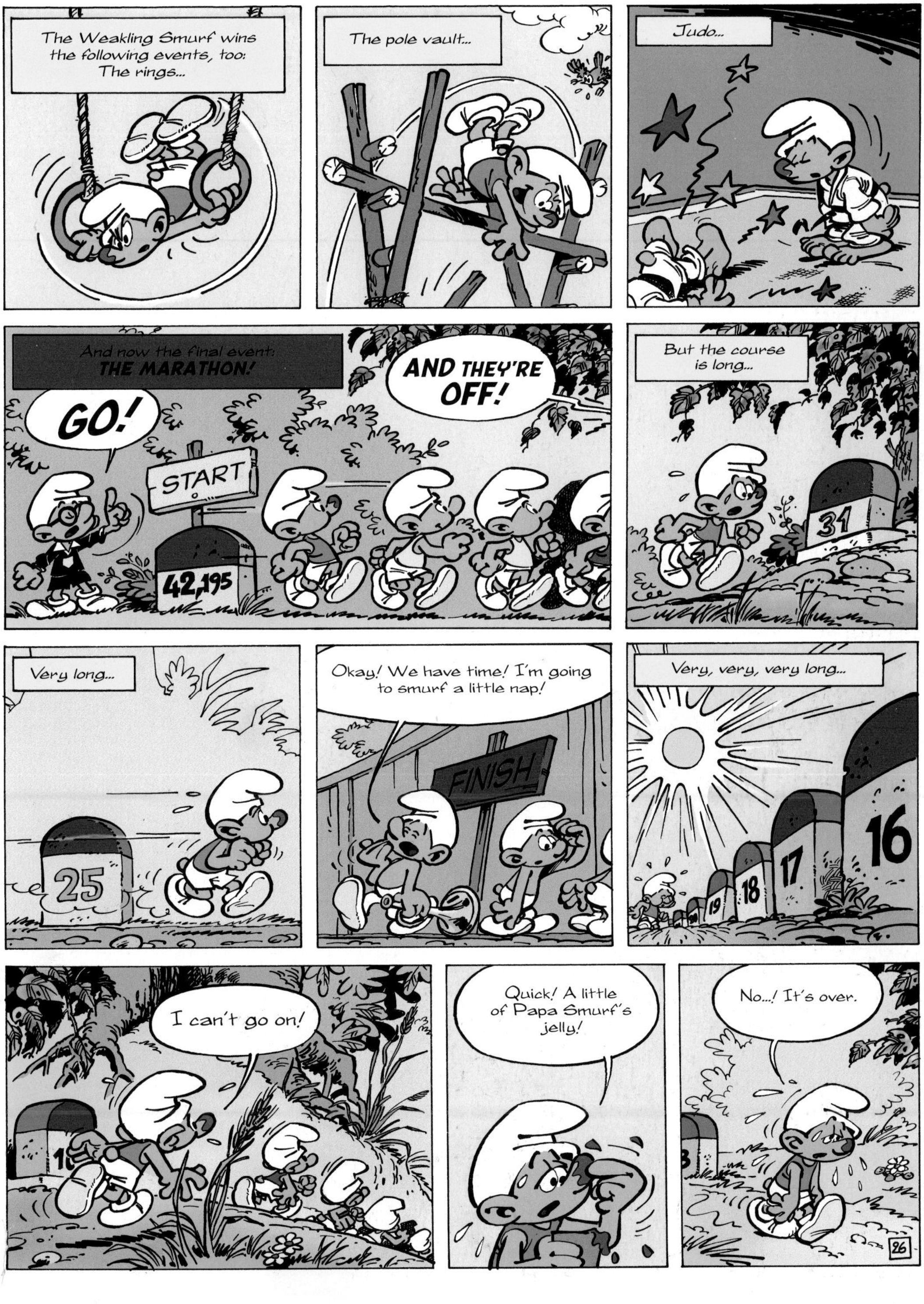

The Weakling Smurf wins the following events, too: The rings...
The pole vault...
Judo...
And now the final event: **THE MARATHON!**
GO!
START
42,195
AND THEY'RE OFF!
But the course is long...
31
Very long...
25
Okay! We have time! I'm going to smurf a little nap!
FINISH
Very, very, very long...
16
17
18
19
I can't go on!
Quick! A little of Papa Smurf's jelly!
No...! It's over.
26

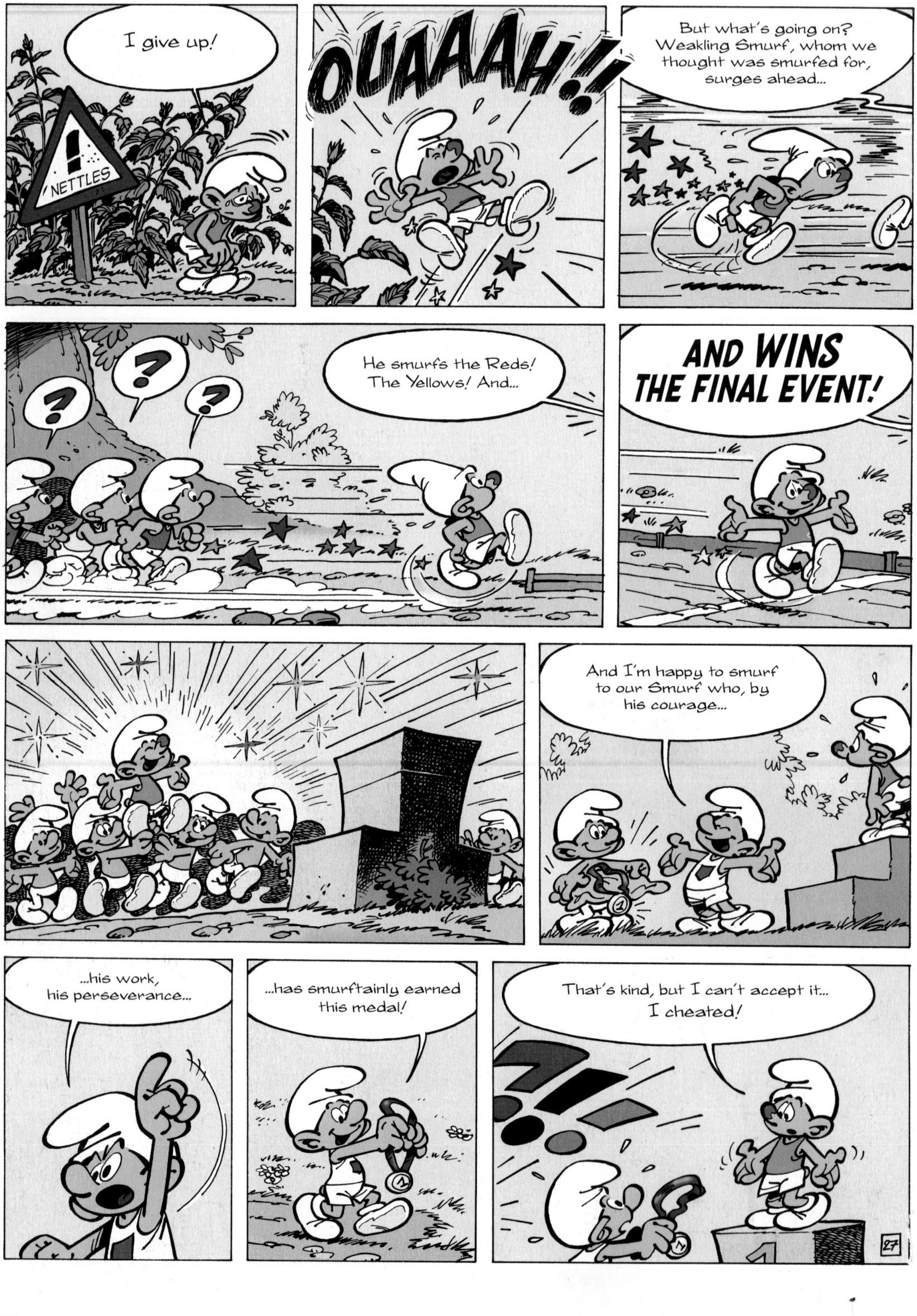

I give up!
NETTLES
OUAAAH!!
But what's going on? Weakling Smurf, whom we thought was smurfed for, surges ahead...
He smurfs the Reds! The Yellows! And...
AND WINS THE FINAL EVENT!
And I'm happy to smurf to our Smurf who, by his courage...
...his work, his perseverance...
...has smurftainly earned this medal!
That's kind, but I can't accept it... I cheated!
27

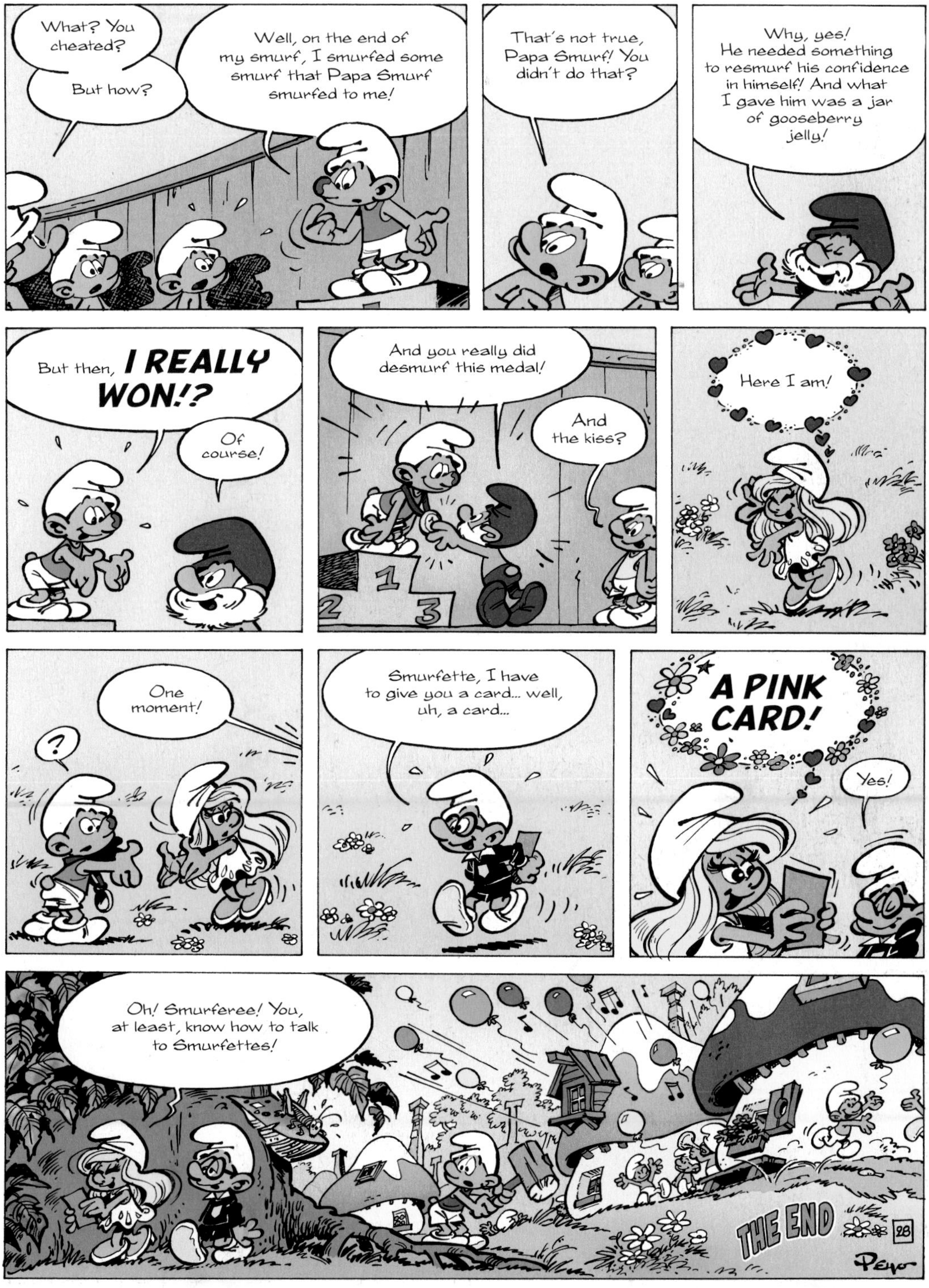
What? You cheated?
But how?
Well, on the end of my smurf, I smurfed some smurf that Papa Smurf smurfed to me!
That's not true, Papa Smurf! You didn't do that?
Why, yes! He needed something to resmurf his confidence in himself! And what I gave him was a jar of gooseberry jelly!
But then, I REALLY WON!?
Of course!
And you really did desmurf this medal!
And the kiss?
Here I am!
?
One moment!
Smurfette, I have to give you a card... well, uh, a card...
A PINK CARD!
Yes!
Oh! Smurferee! You, at least, know how to talk to Smurfettes!
THE END
28
Peyo

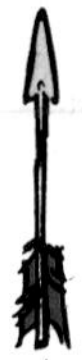

MORE SMURF OLYMPICS

As Papa Smurf put it so well, smurfing isn't what's important, participating is–
And it's in order to form the mind as much as the muscles (*smurf sano in corpore smurfo*) that the Smurfs devotes themselves to the glorious uncertainty of smurf...

Peyo ★ Y. Delporte

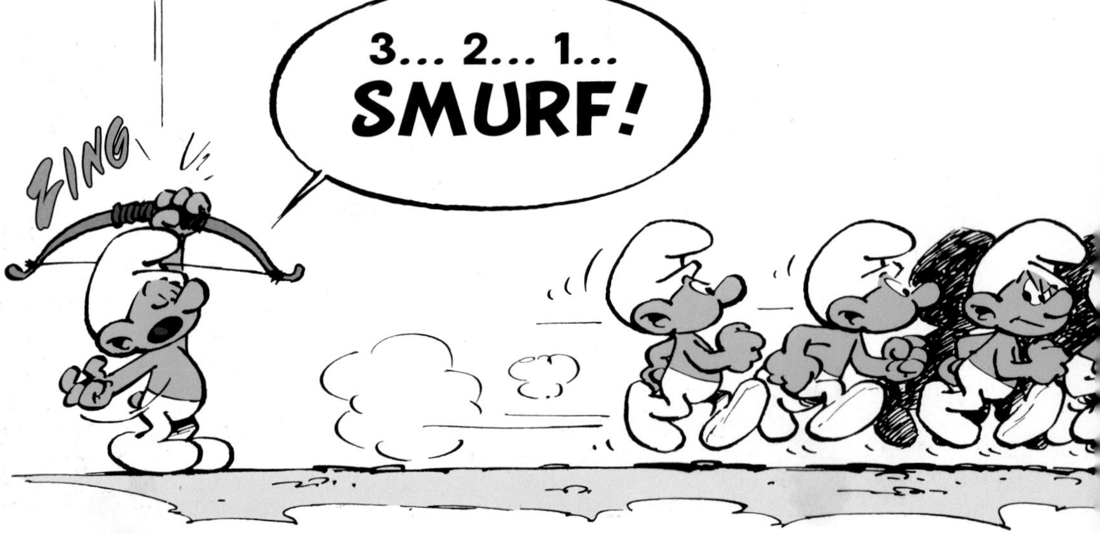
3... 2... 1...
SMURF!
ZING

ARISE, YE SMURFLIFTERS OF THE WORLD!

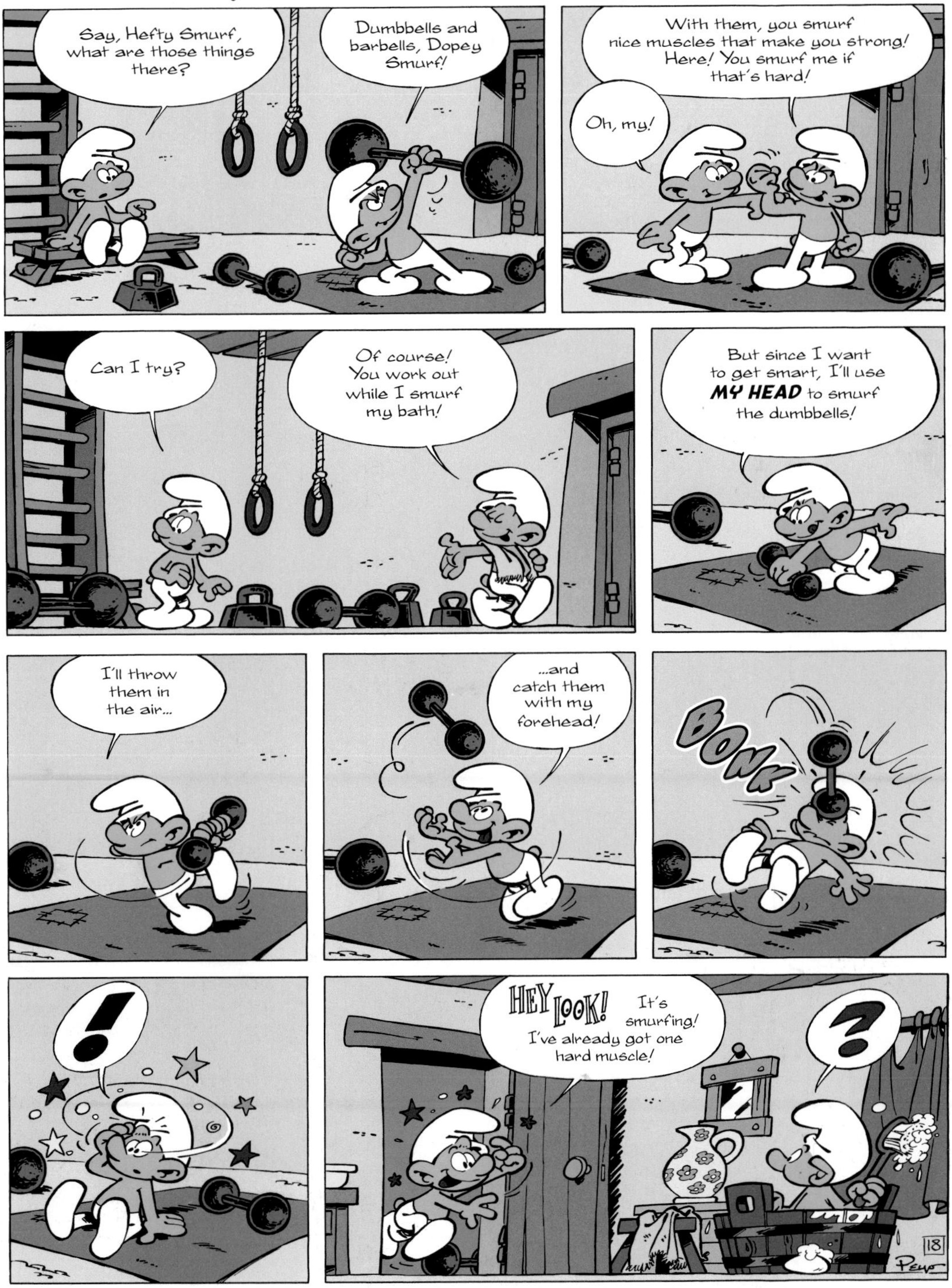

Say, Hefty Smurf, what are those things there?
Dumbbells and barbells, Dopey Smurf!
With them, you smurf nice muscles that make you strong! Here! You smurf me if that's hard!
Oh, my!
Can I try?
Of course! You work out while I smurf my bath!
But since I want to get smart, I'll use **MY HEAD** to smurf the dumbbells!
I'll throw them in the air...
...and catch them with my forehead!
BONK
!
HEY LOOK! It's smurfing! I've already got one hard muscle!
?
18
Peyo

SMURFÉADOR, PRENDS GA-A-A-ARDE...

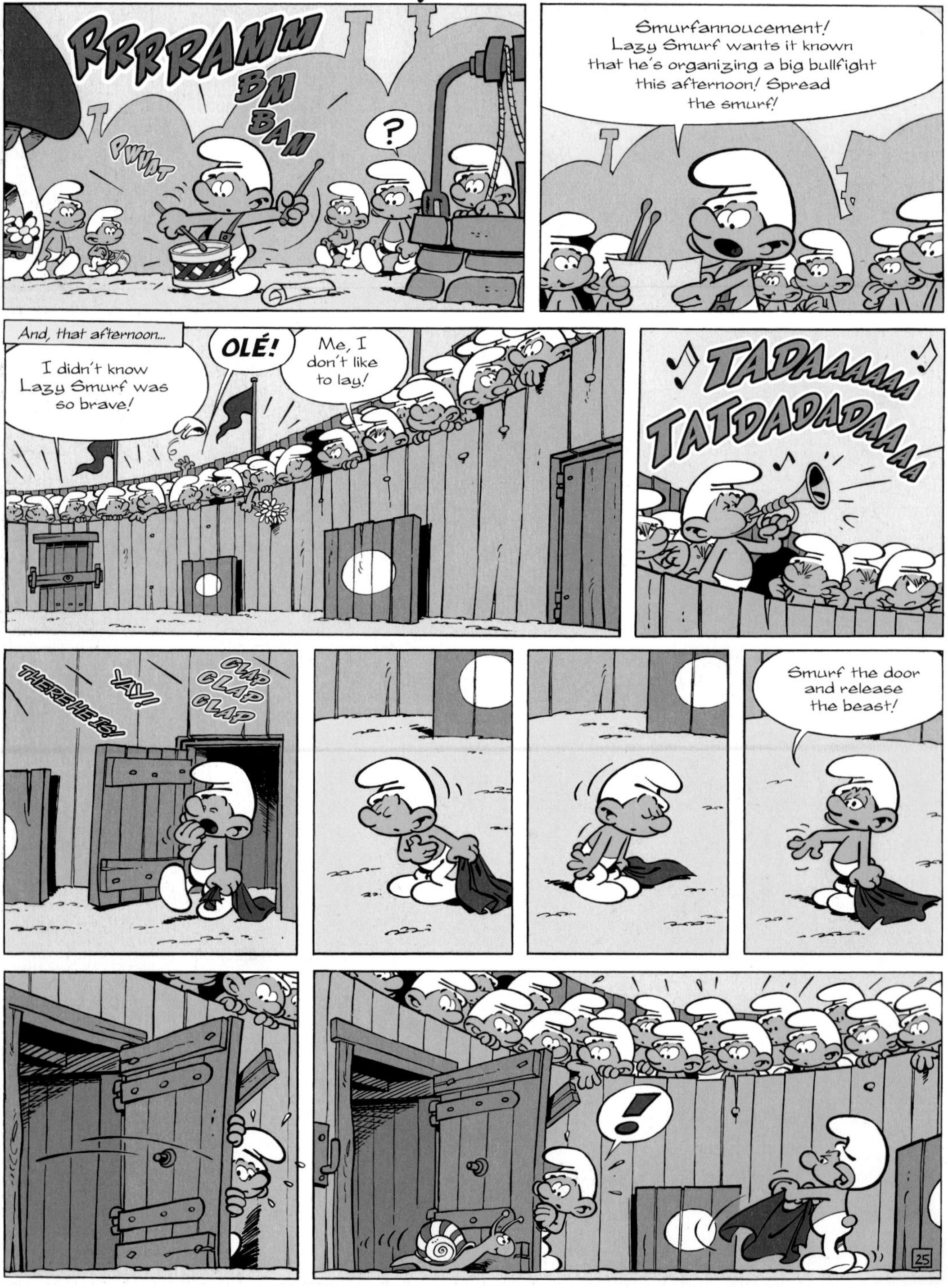

RRRRAMM
BM BAM
PWHAT
?
Smurfannoucement! Lazy Smurf wants it known that he's organizing a big bullfight this afternoon! Spread the smurf!
And, that afternoon...
I didn't know Lazy Smurf was so brave!
OLÉ!
Me, I don't like to lay!
TADAAAAAA TATDADADAAAA
THERE HE IS!
YAY!
CLAP CLAP CLAP
Smurf the door and release the beast!
!
25

SMURFING BY A THREAD.

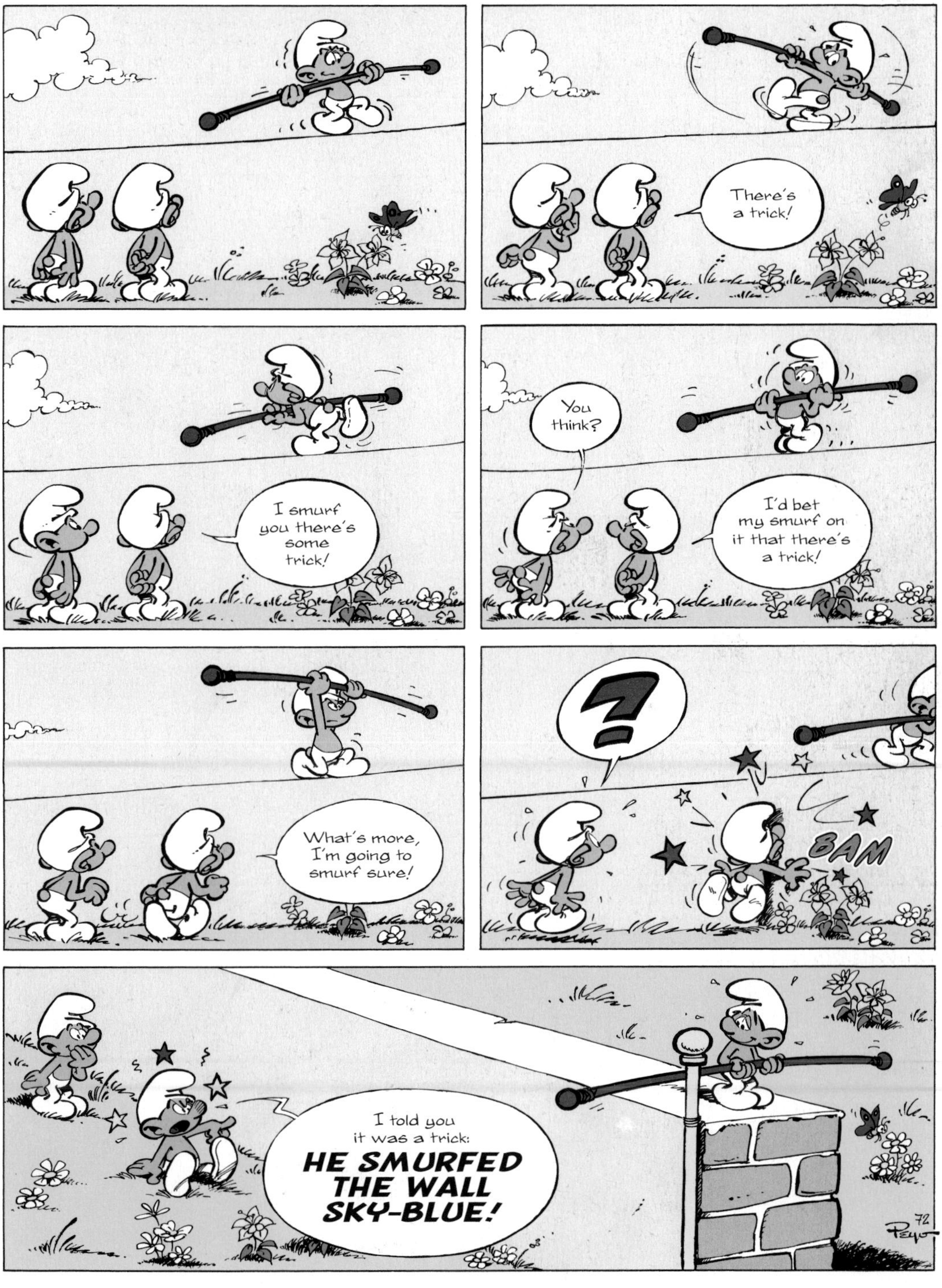
There's a trick!
I smurf you there's some trick!
You think?
I'd bet my smurf on it that there's a trick!
What's more, I'm going to smurf sure!
?
BAM
I told you it was a trick: HE SMURFED THE WALL SKY-BLUE!
Peyo 72

DIFFERENT STROKES FOR DIFFERENT SMURFS.

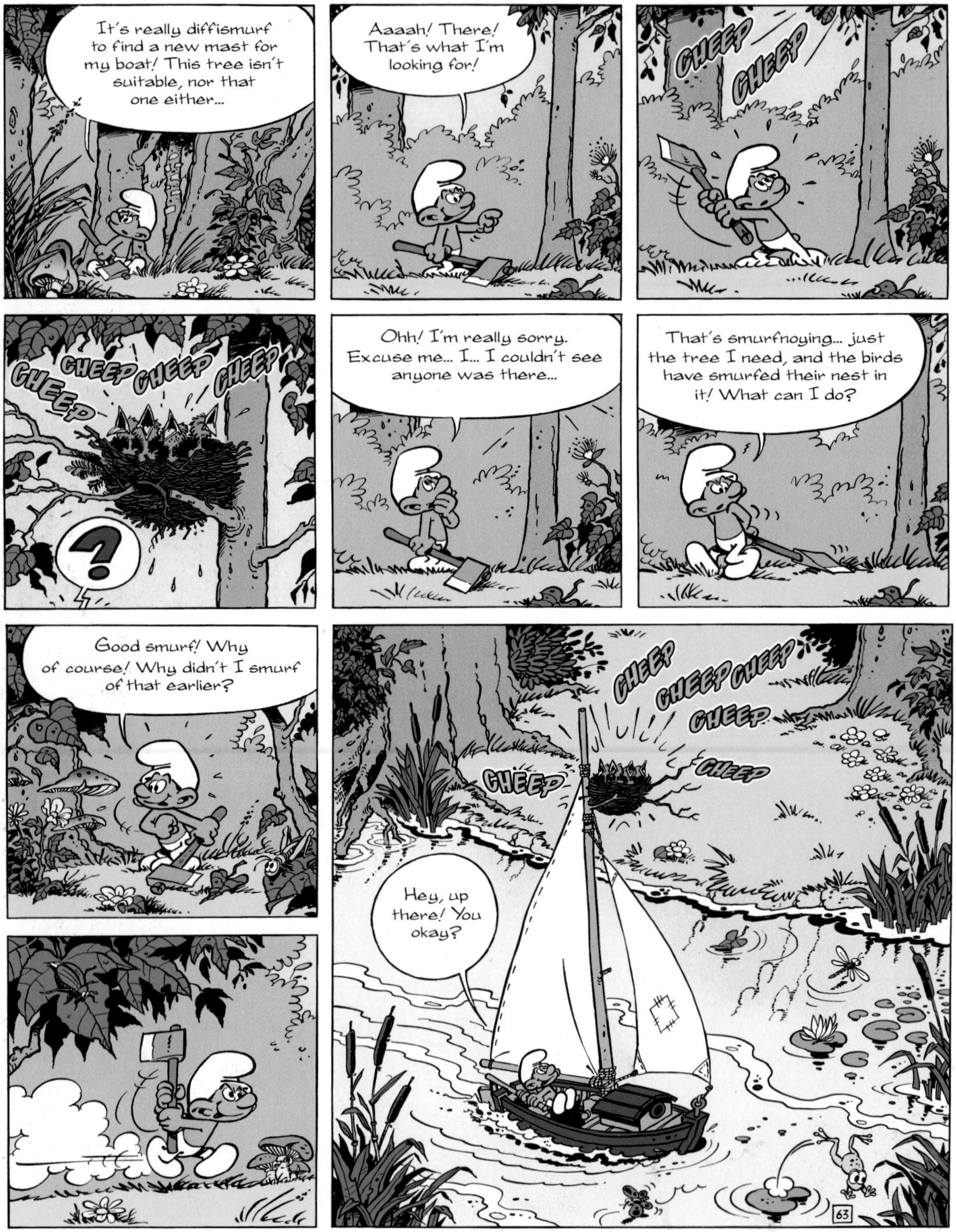

It's really diffismurf to find a new mast for my boat! This tree isn't suitable, nor that one either...
Aaaah! There! That's what I'm looking for!
CHEEP
CHEEP
CHEEP
CHEEP
CHEEP
CHEEP
Ohh! I'm really sorry. Excuse me... I... I couldn't see anyone was there...
That's smurfnoying... just the tree I need, and the birds have smurfed their nest in it! What can I do?
Good smurf! Why of course! Why didn't I smurf of that earlier?
CHEEP
CHEEP
CHEEP
CHEEP
CHEEP
CHEEP
Hey, up there! You okay?
63

UNLUCKY IN LOVE, LUCKY AT SMURFS.

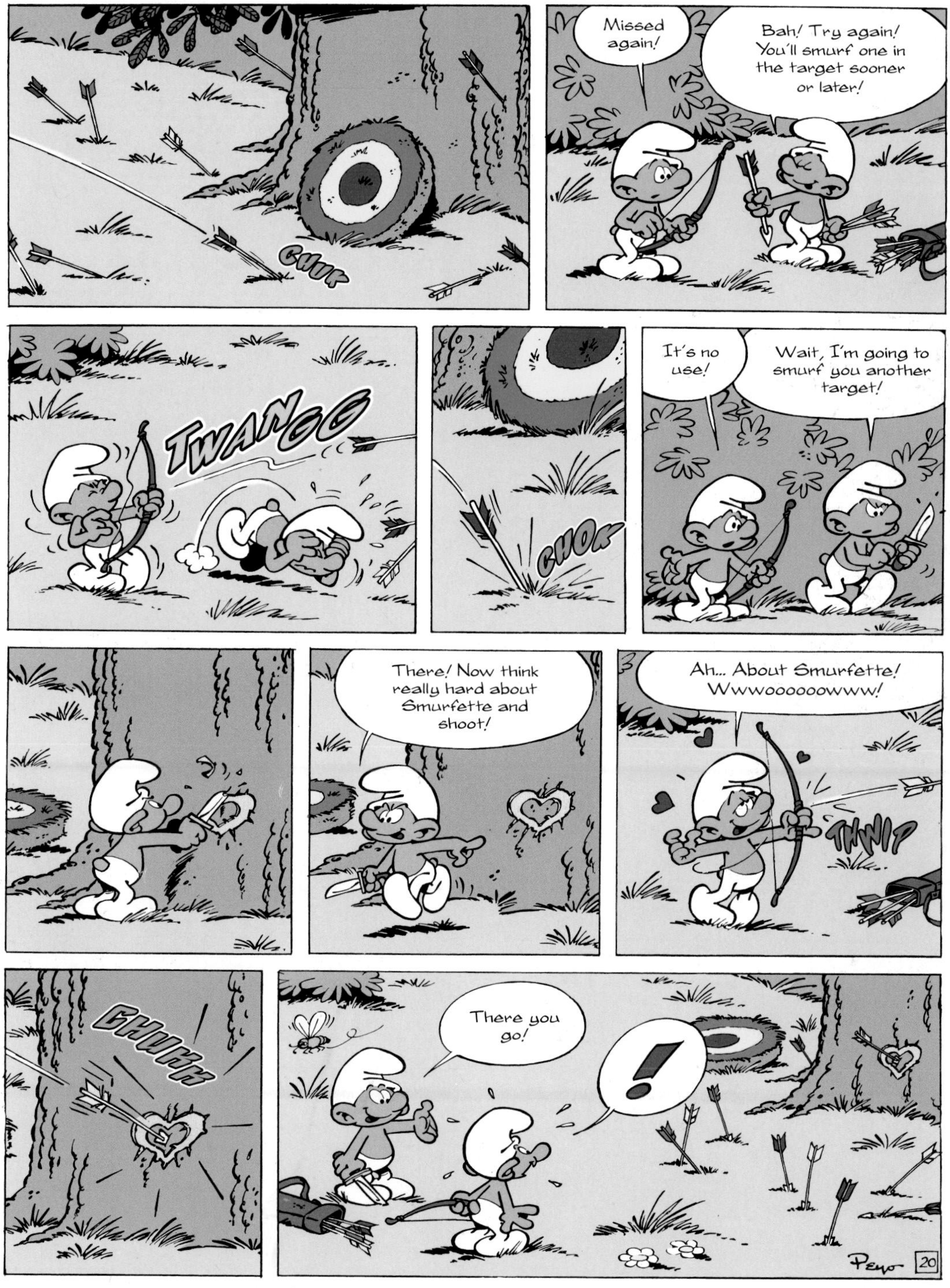

CHUK
Missed again!
Bah! Try again! You'll smurf one in the target sooner or later!
TWANGG
CHOK
It's no use!
Wait, I'm going to smurf you another target!
There! Now think really hard about Smurfette and shoot!
Ah... About Smurfette! Wwwoooooowww!
THWIP
CHUKK
There you go!
!
Peyo
20

ONLY ONE SMURF OF THE STORY

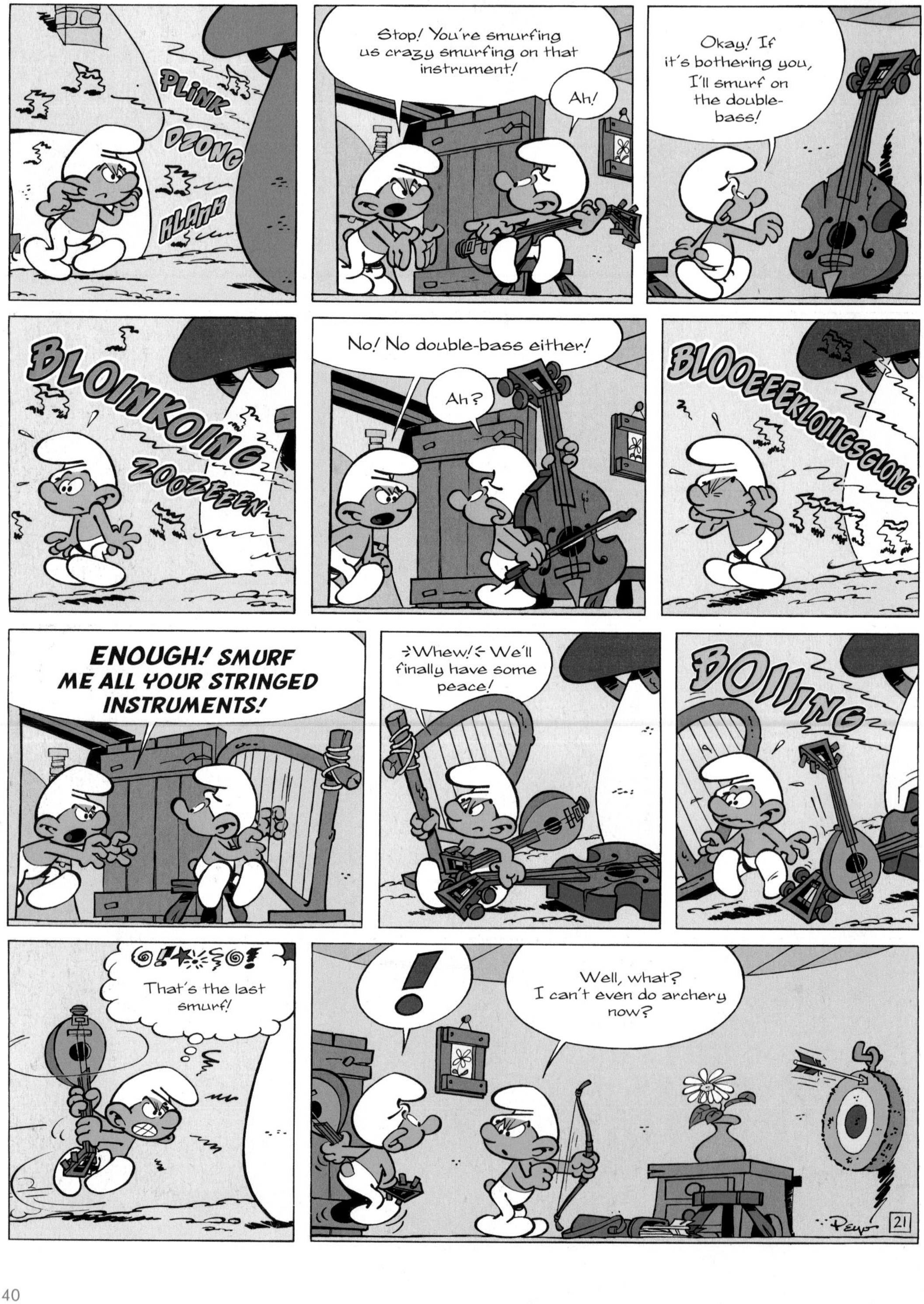

PLINK
DZONG
KLANK
Stop! You're smurfing us crazy smurfing on that instrument!
Ah!
Okay! If it's bothering you, I'll smurf on the double-bass!
BLOINKOING
ZOOZEEEN
No! No double-bass either!
Ah?
BLOOEEEKLOIIGSGLONG
ENOUGH! SMURF ME ALL YOUR STRINGED INSTRUMENTS!
Whew! We'll finally have some peace!
BOIIING
That's the last smurf!
!
Well, what? I can't even do archery now?
Peyo
21

USING ALL THE AVAILABLE MEANS

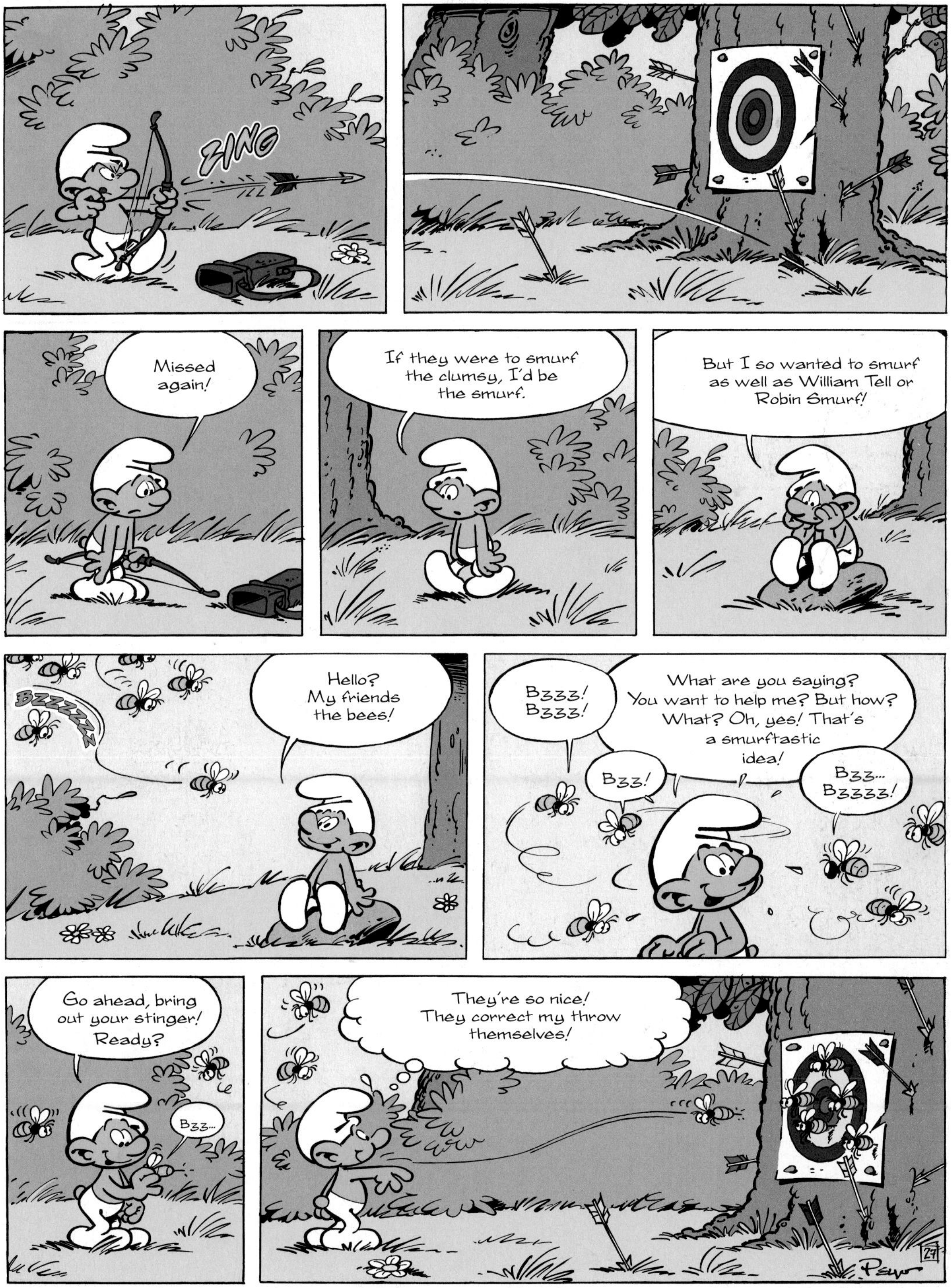
ZING
Missed again!
If they were to smurf the clumsy, I'd be the smurf.
But I so wanted to smurf as well as William Tell or Robin Smurf!
BZZZZZZZ
Hello? My friends the bees!
Bzzz! Bzzz!
What are you saying? You want to help me? But how? What? Oh, yes! That's a smurftastic idea!
Bzz!
Bzz... Bzzzz!
Go ahead, bring out your stinger! Ready?
Bzz...
They're so nice! They correct my throw themselves!
27
Peyo

TALK IS SMURF

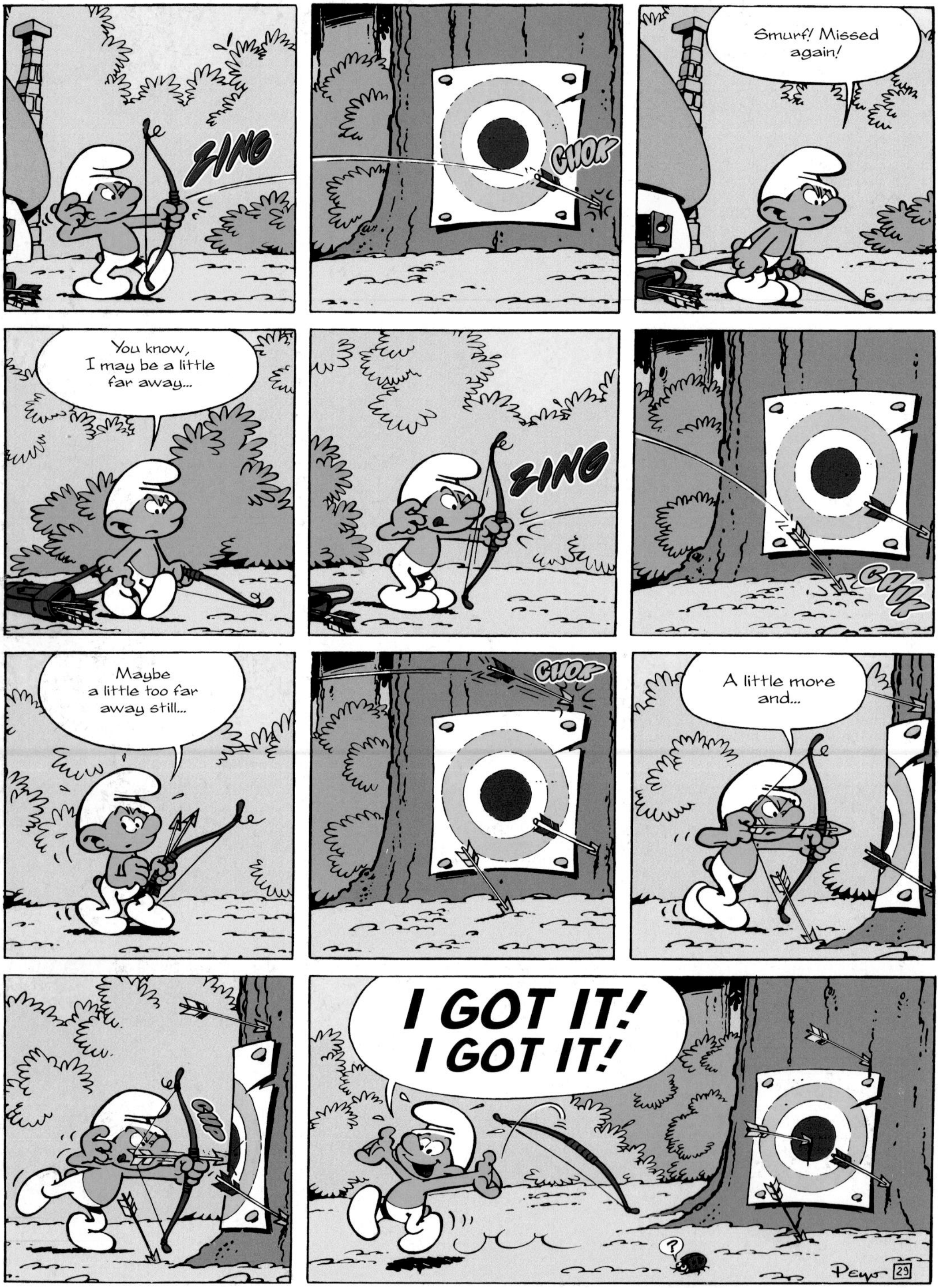

ZING
CHOK
Smurf! Missed again!
You know, I may be a little far away...
ZING
CHUK
Maybe a little too far away still...
CHOK
A little more and...
GLIP
I GOT IT! I GOT IT!
?
Peyo
29

MAKING A SILK PURSE OUT OF A SMURF'S EAR

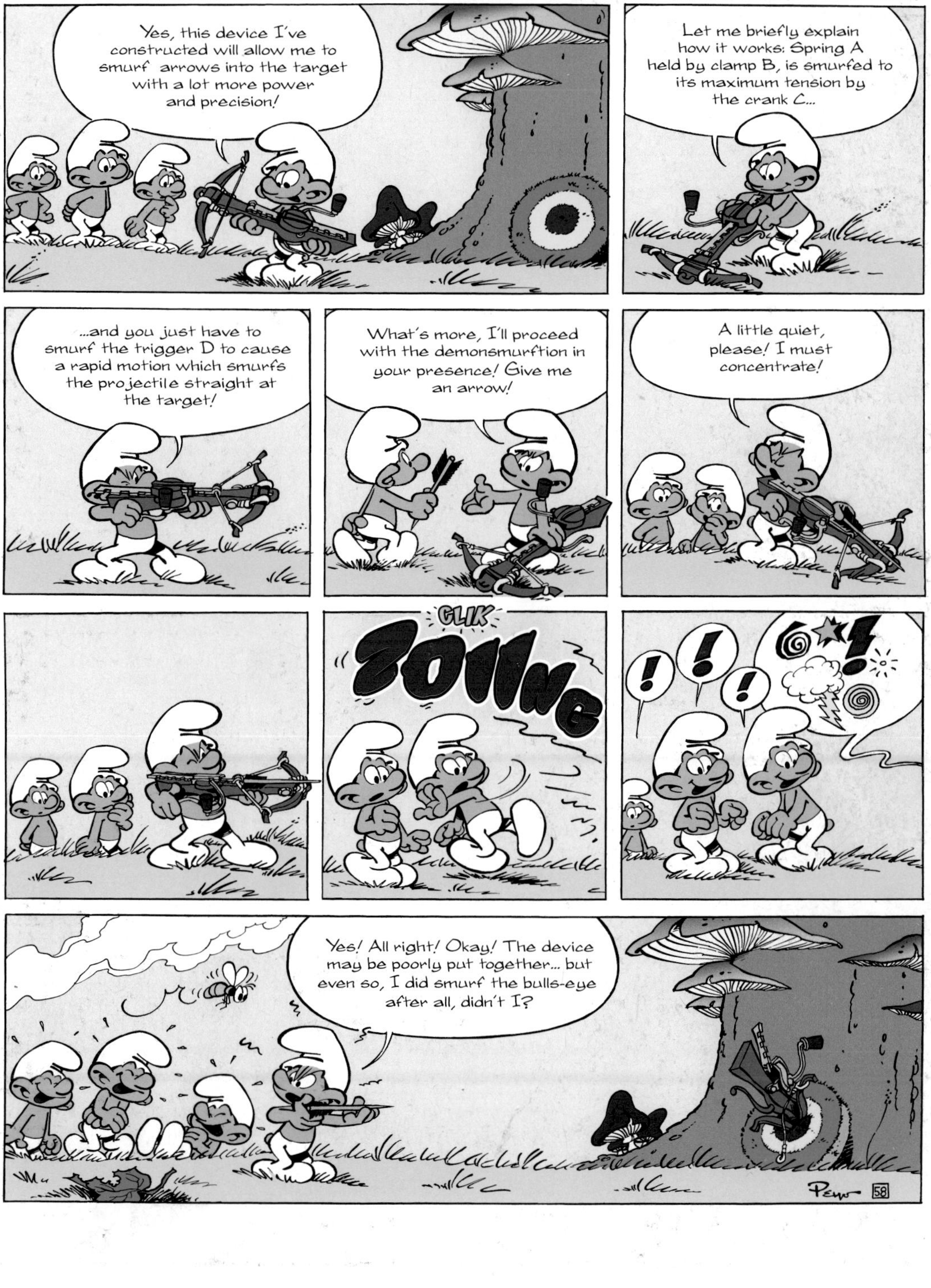
Yes, this device I've constructed will allow me to smurf arrows into the target with a lot more power and precision!
Let me briefly explain how it works: Spring A held by clamp B, is smurfed to its maximum tension by the crank C...
...and you just have to smurf the trigger D to cause a rapid motion which smurfs the projectile straight at the target!
What's more, I'll proceed with the demonsmurftion in your presence! Give me an arrow!
A little quiet, please! I must concentrate!
CLIK
ZOIING
!
!
!
Yes! All right! Okay! The device may be poorly put together... but even so, I did smurf the bulls-eye after all, didn't I?
Peyo 58

STILL SMURFS RUN DEEP

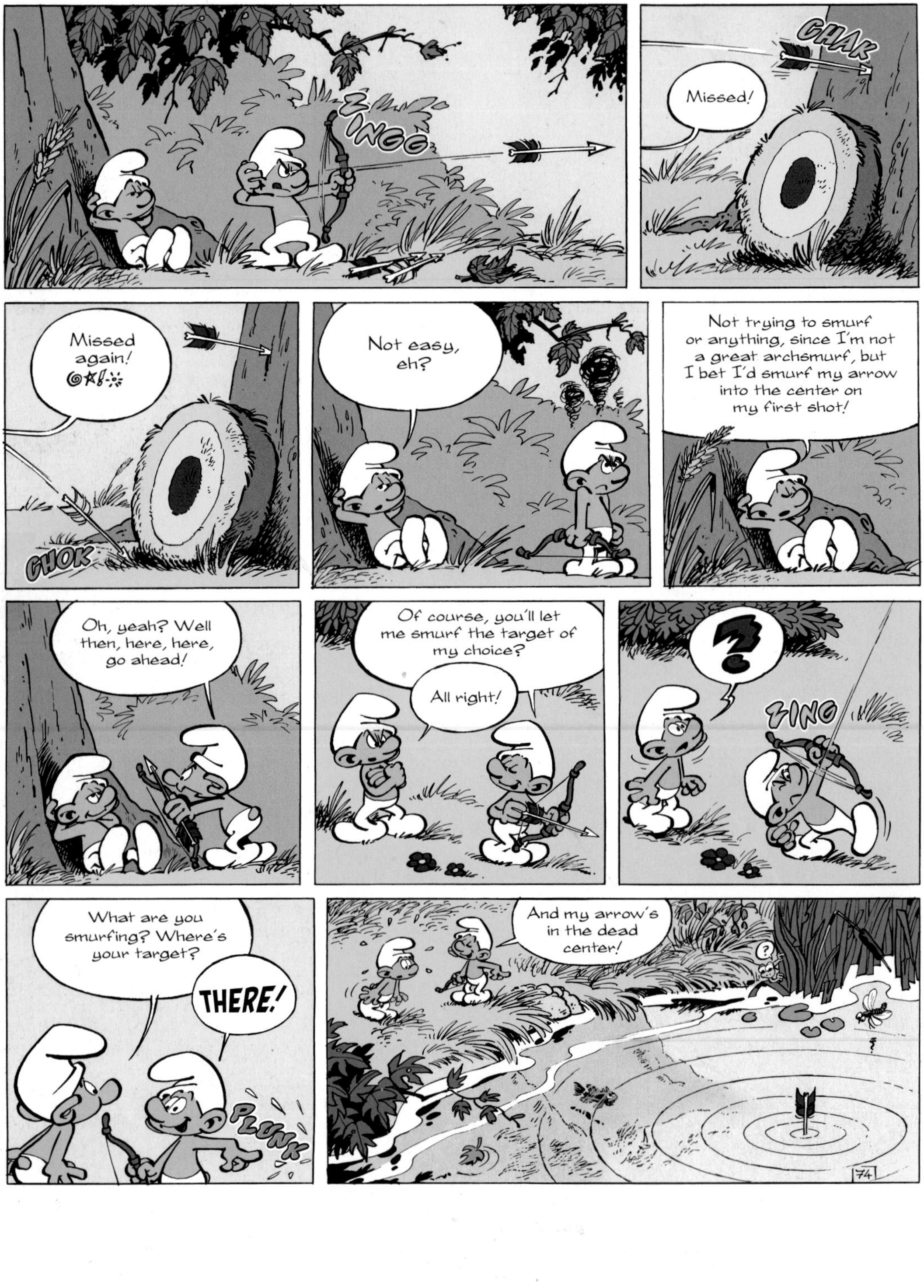
ZINGG
CHAK
Missed!
Missed again! @*!:*
CHOK
Not easy, eh?
Not trying to smurf or anything, since I'm not a great archsmurf, but I bet I'd smurf my arrow into the center on my first shot!
Oh, yeah? Well then, here, here, go ahead!
Of course, you'll let me smurf the target of my choice?
All right!
?
ZING
What are you smurfing? Where's your target?
THERE!
PLUNK
And my arrow's in the dead center!
?
74

YOU HAVE TO HAVE MORE THAN ONE SMURF ON YOUR BOW

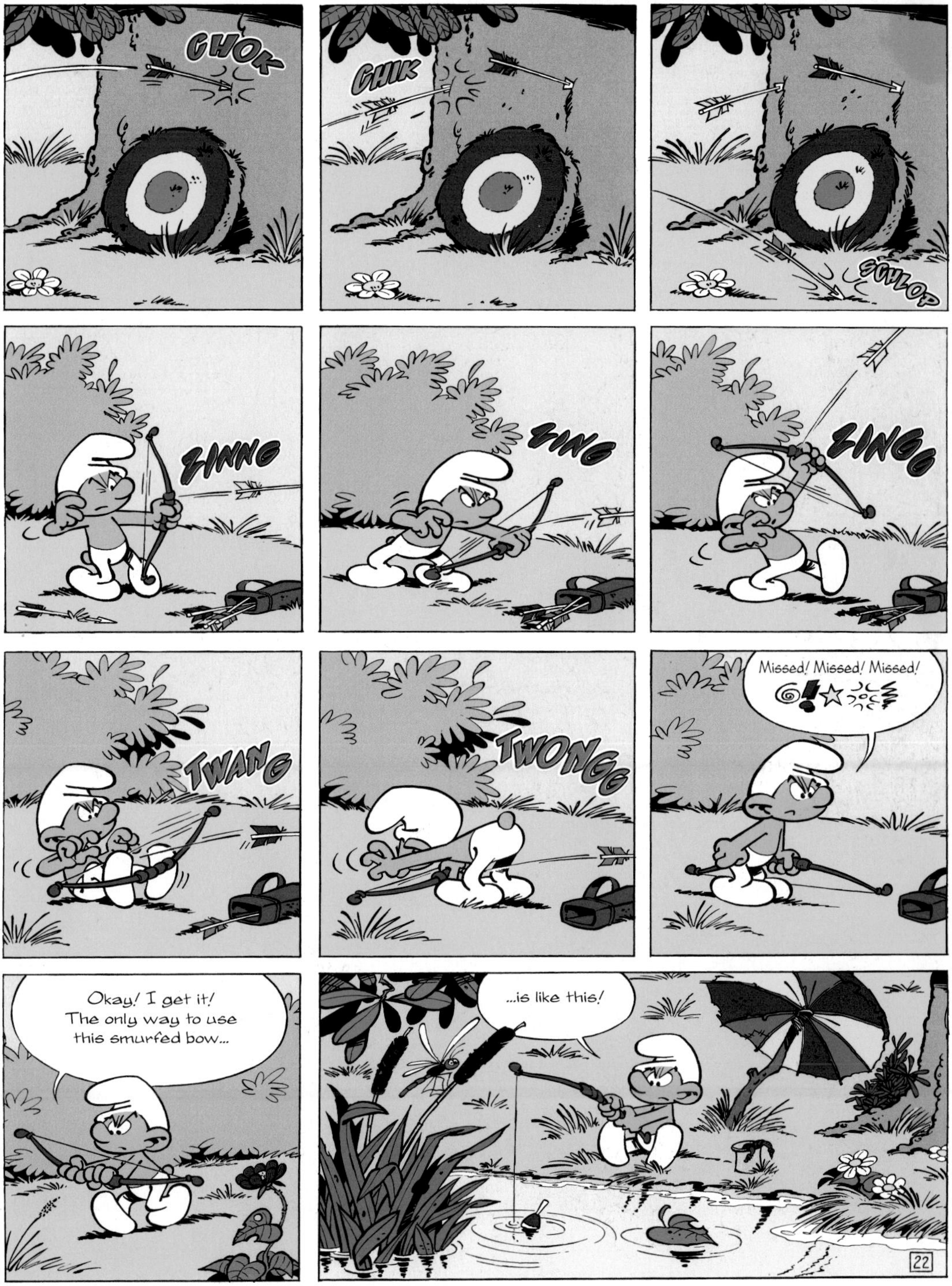
CHOK
CHIK
SCHLOP
ZINNG
ZING
ZINGG
TWANG
TWONGG
Missed! Missed! Missed!
Okay! I get it! The only way to use this smurfed bow...
...is like this!
22

THE SMURF THAT BROKE THE CAMEL'S BACK

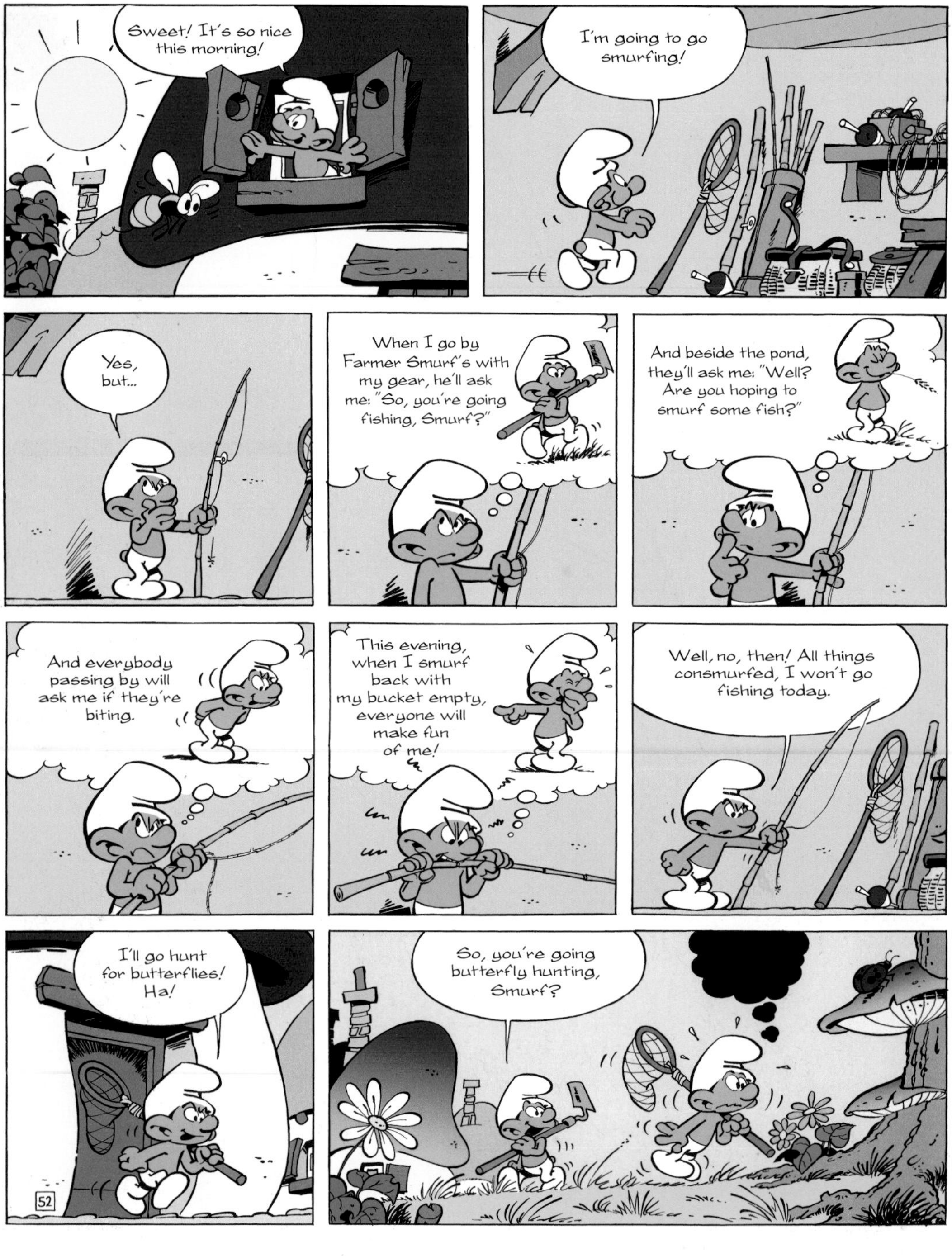

Sweet! It's so nice this morning!
I'm going to go smurfing!
Yes, but...
When I go by Farmer Smurf's with my gear, he'll ask me: "So, you're going fishing, Smurf?"
And beside the pond, they'll ask me: "Well? Are you hoping to smurf some fish?"
And everybody passing by will ask me if they're biting.
This evening, when I smurf back with my bucket empty, everyone will make fun of me!
Well, no, then! All things consmurfed, I won't go fishing today.
I'll go hunt for butterflies! Ha!
52
So, you're going butterfly hunting, Smurf?

A ROLLING SMURF GATHERS NO MOSS

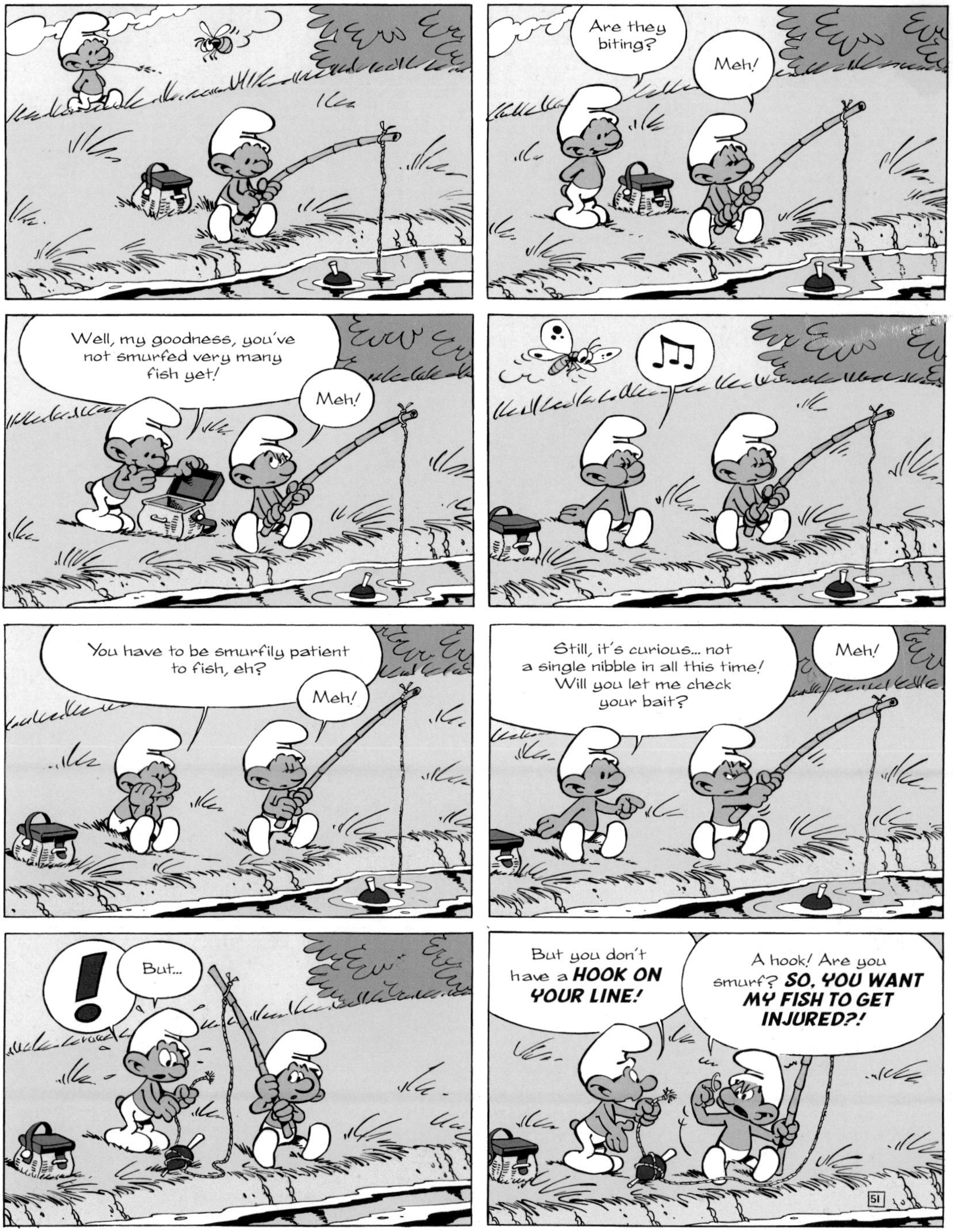

Are they biting?
Meh!
Well, my goodness, you've not smurfed very many fish yet!
Meh!
You have to be smurfily patient to fish, eh?
Meh!
Still, it's curious... not a single nibble in all this time! Will you let me check your bait?
Meh!
!
But...
But you don't have a **HOOK ON YOUR LINE!**
A hook! Are you smurf? **SO, YOU WANT MY FISH TO GET INJURED?!**
51

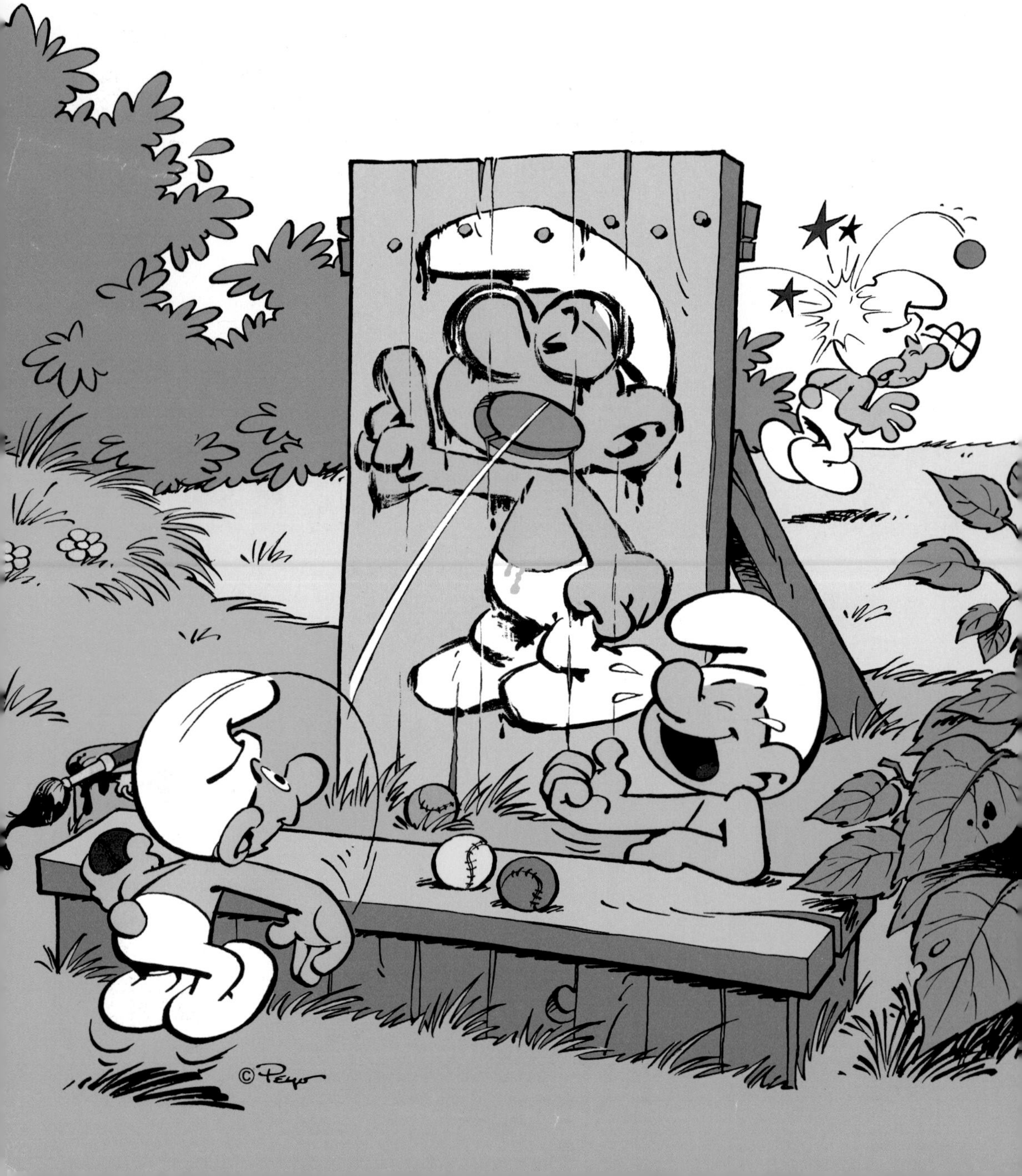
©Peyo

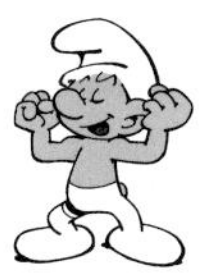

the SMURFS COMIC STRIPS BY Peyo

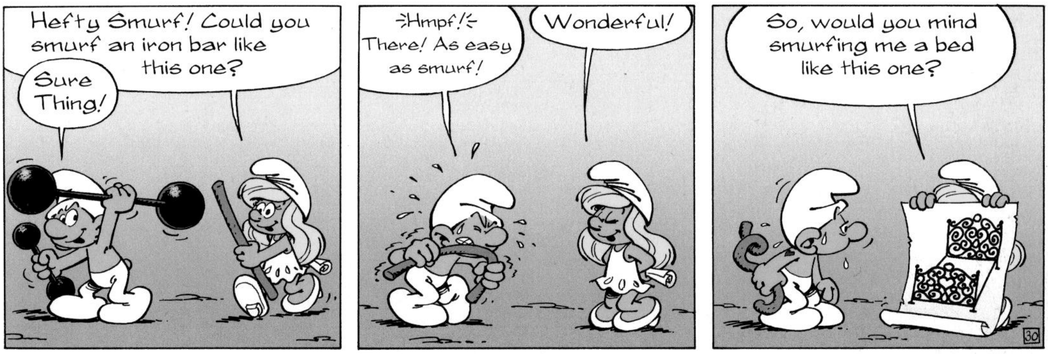

Hefty Smurf! Could you smurf an iron bar like this one?
Sure Thing!
Hmpf!
There! As easy as smurf!
Wonderful!
So, would you mind smurfing me a bed like this one?
30

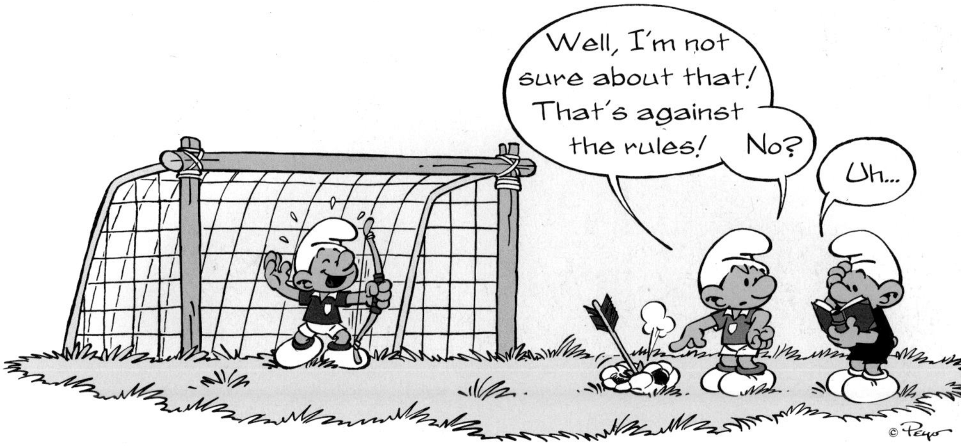

Well, I'm not sure about that! That's against the rules!
No?
Uh...
© Peyo

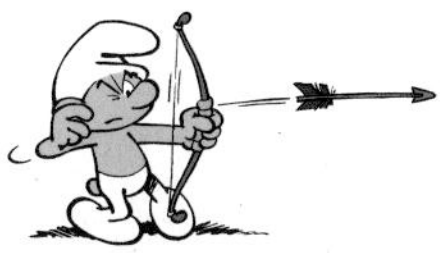

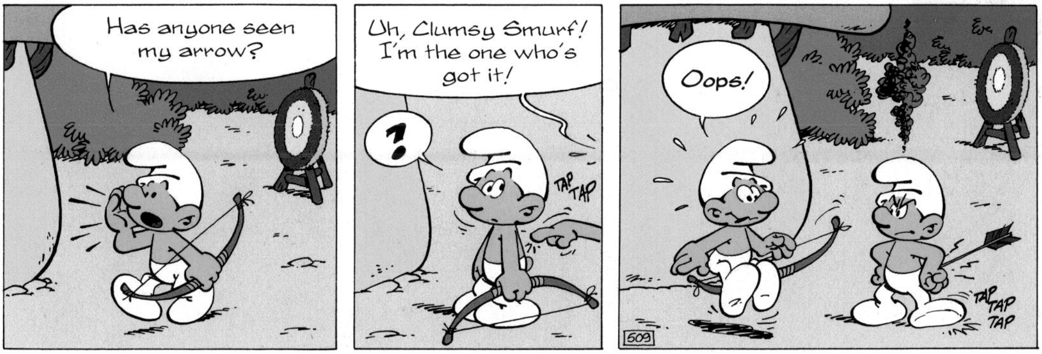

Has anyone seen my arrow?
Uh, Clumsy Smurf! I'm the one who's got it!
?
TAP TAP
Oops!
TAP TAP TAP
509

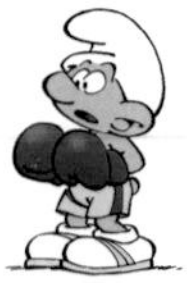

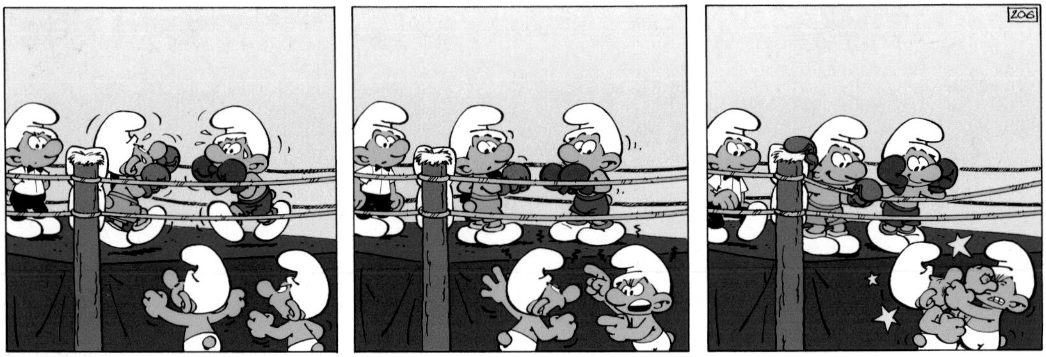
206

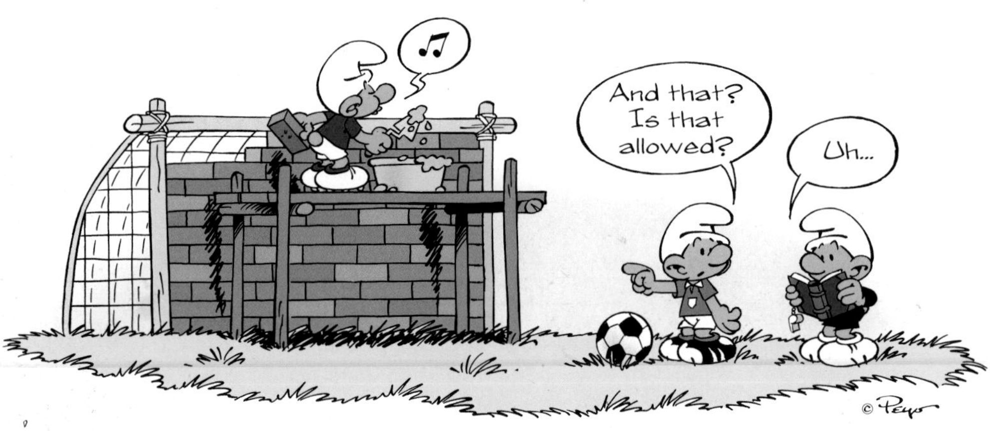
And that? Is that allowed?
Uh...
© Peyo

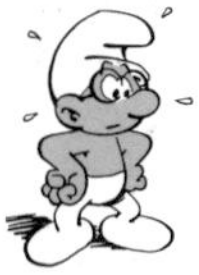

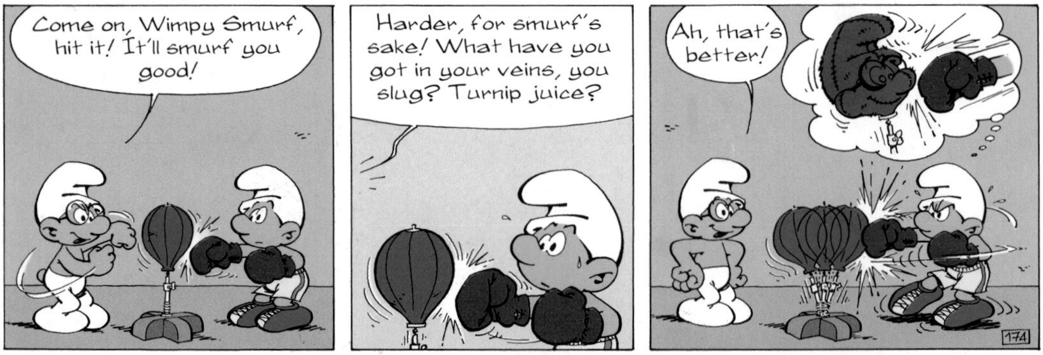
Come on, Wimpy Smurf, hit it! It'll smurf you good!
Harder, for smurf's sake! What have you got in your veins, you slug? Turnip juice?
Ah, that's better!
171

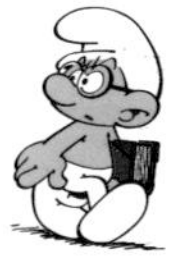

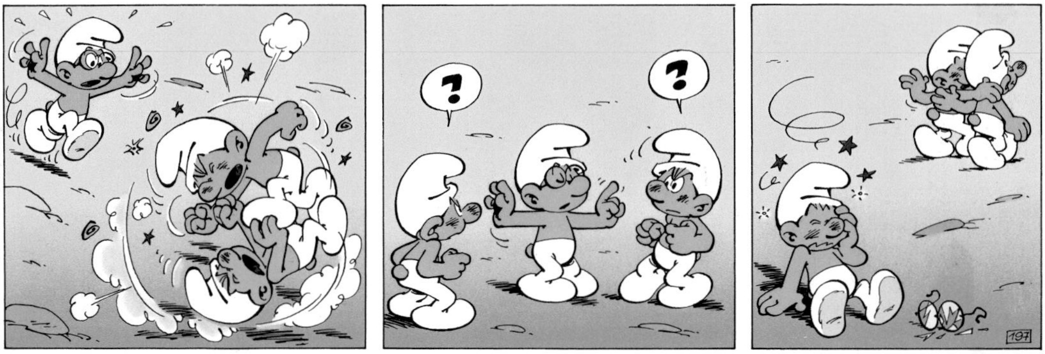
?
?
197

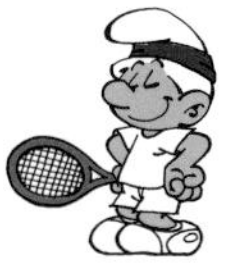

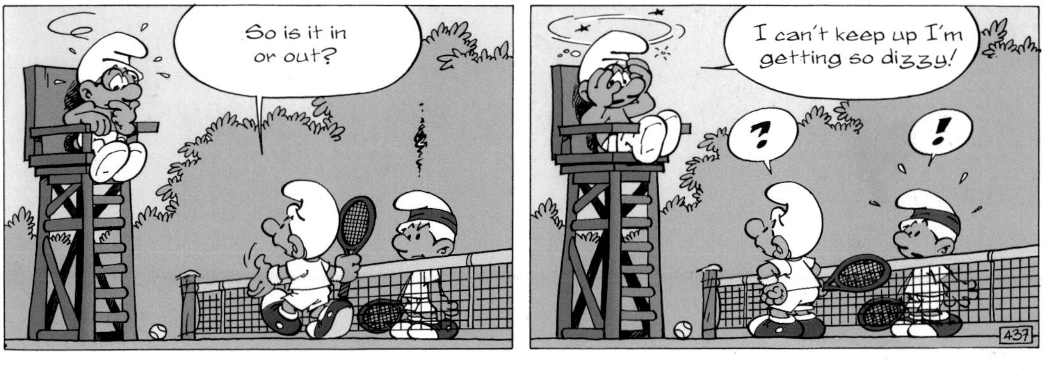
So is it in or out?
I can't keep up I'm getting so dizzy!
?
!
437

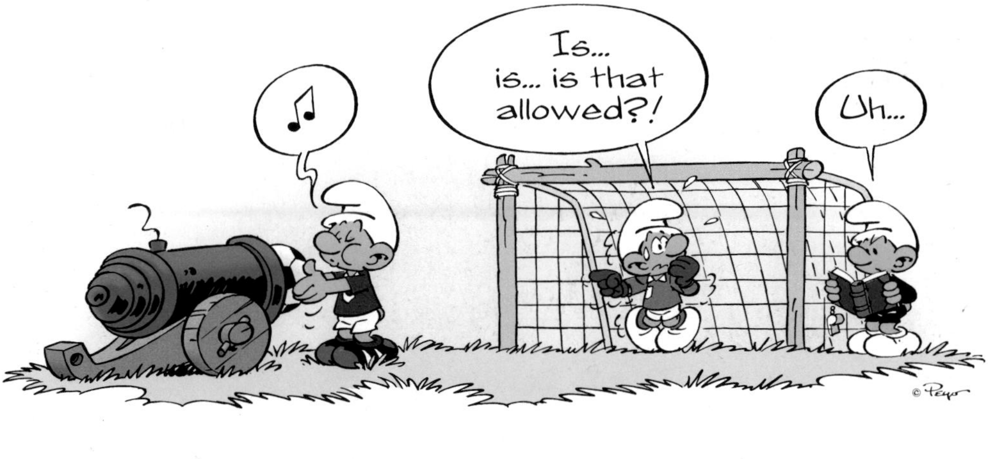
♫
Is... is... is that allowed?!
Uh...
© Peyo

WATCH OUT FOR PAPERCUTZ™

Associate Smurf Michael Petranek

Welcome to the especially energetic eleventh SMURFS graphic novel by Peyo from Papercutz, the tiny but highly competitive publisher of great graphic novels for all ages. I'm Jim Salicrup, your out-of-shape Smurf-in-Chief. Fortunately, thanks to Associate Smurf Michael Petranek, we've got an able-bodied person to do most of the heavy lifting around here.

As Smurf-in-Chief, my main responsibility is to make sure each and every Papercutz edition of THE SMURFS is as Smurfy as possible. That's not too difficult when you're starting out with such Smurftacular material as the original Smurfs comics created by Peyo, and you have such talented and devoted folks such as Lettering Smurfette Janice Chiang (see THE SMURFS #9), Smurfic Designer Adam Grano (See SMURFS #8), and Smurflator Joe Johnson (See SMURFS #10) on your team. But holding it all together, and patiently and politely helping everyone to do their work as painlessly as possible is our very own Associate Smurf Michael Petranek.

Despite having to endure my countless Gargamelian rants, Michael is able to maintain focus on making sure each volume is assembled properly and with special care. You'd be surprised what could potentially go wrong! Azrael could be the wrong shade of orange! Papa Smurf could be saying dialogue intended for the Smurfette! Brainy Smurf could open a present from Jokey Smurf that doesn't explode! And, if on those rare occasions a minor boo-boo does slip through, it's Michael who makes sure it's corrected in the next printing.

But who is this mysterious Mr. Petranek? Michael Petranek denies that he was born in the Smurf's Village, and insists he was born in someplace called Dallas, Texas. It was there that Michael began his intense study of the comicbook artform by grabbing every comicbook he could get his hands on… legally. He also claims to play several musical instruments, but then again, so does Harmony Smurf. He has also directed theatrical plays and short films, so he truly is a very creative guy. But despite his closeness to Broadway and to several major comicbook publishers in New York City, Michael still gets homesick for his family, including his "little brother," an eighty-pound yellow lab named "Zeus."

But what's really most impressive about Michael is how much he cares about every detail of putting Papercutz graphic novels and comics together. For example, just by hanging around the palatial Papercutz offices and asking the right questions, he's managed to teach himself all sorts of stuff on his Mac (I believe the Smurfs themselves are three macs tall, right?). Thus, he's even lettered the three pages of Smurfs comic strips featured in this very volume. And I can't forget how considerate he was earlier this year when he scheduled my time at the Papercutz booth at the New York Comic-Con so that I would be free to see a few panels. I really appreciated the chance to see such comicbook legends as Stan Lee and Joe Simon. Thanks again, Michael.

Yes, thanks to Michael's calm and friendly manner, not only do we get a lot done in as stress-free an environment as possible, but we can actually have fun doing it! If only Michael could actually be in the Smurfs Village, he'd be able to keep things happy and fun, unlike what happens there in SMURFS #12 "Smurf Vs. Smurf." To see what I'm talking about, check out the preview on the following pages. Yep, things must've gotten really crazy if Papa Smurf is seeking Gargamel's help! He should be asking Mister Petranek instead!

Smurf you later,

Jim

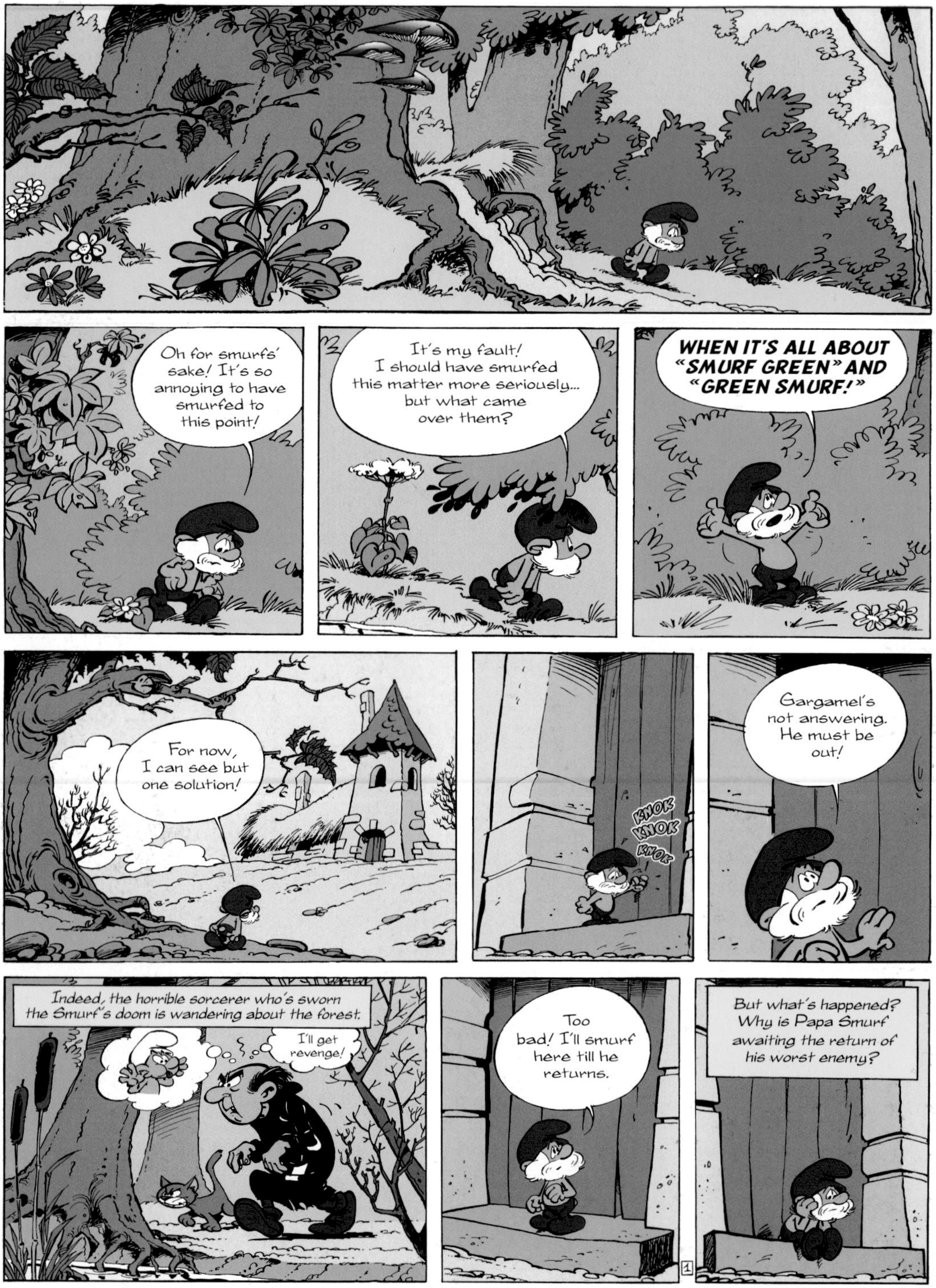
Oh for smurfs' sake! It's so annoying to have smurfed to this point!
It's my fault! I should have smurfed this matter more seriously... but what came over them?
WHEN IT'S ALL ABOUT "SMURF GREEN" AND "GREEN SMURF!"
For now, I can see but one solution!
KNOK KNOK KNOK
Gargamel's not answering. He must be out!
Indeed, the horrible sorcerer who's sworn the Smurf's doom is wandering about the forest.
I'll get revenge!
Too bad! I'll smurf here till he returns.
1
But what's happened? Why is Papa Smurf awaiting the return of his worst enemy?

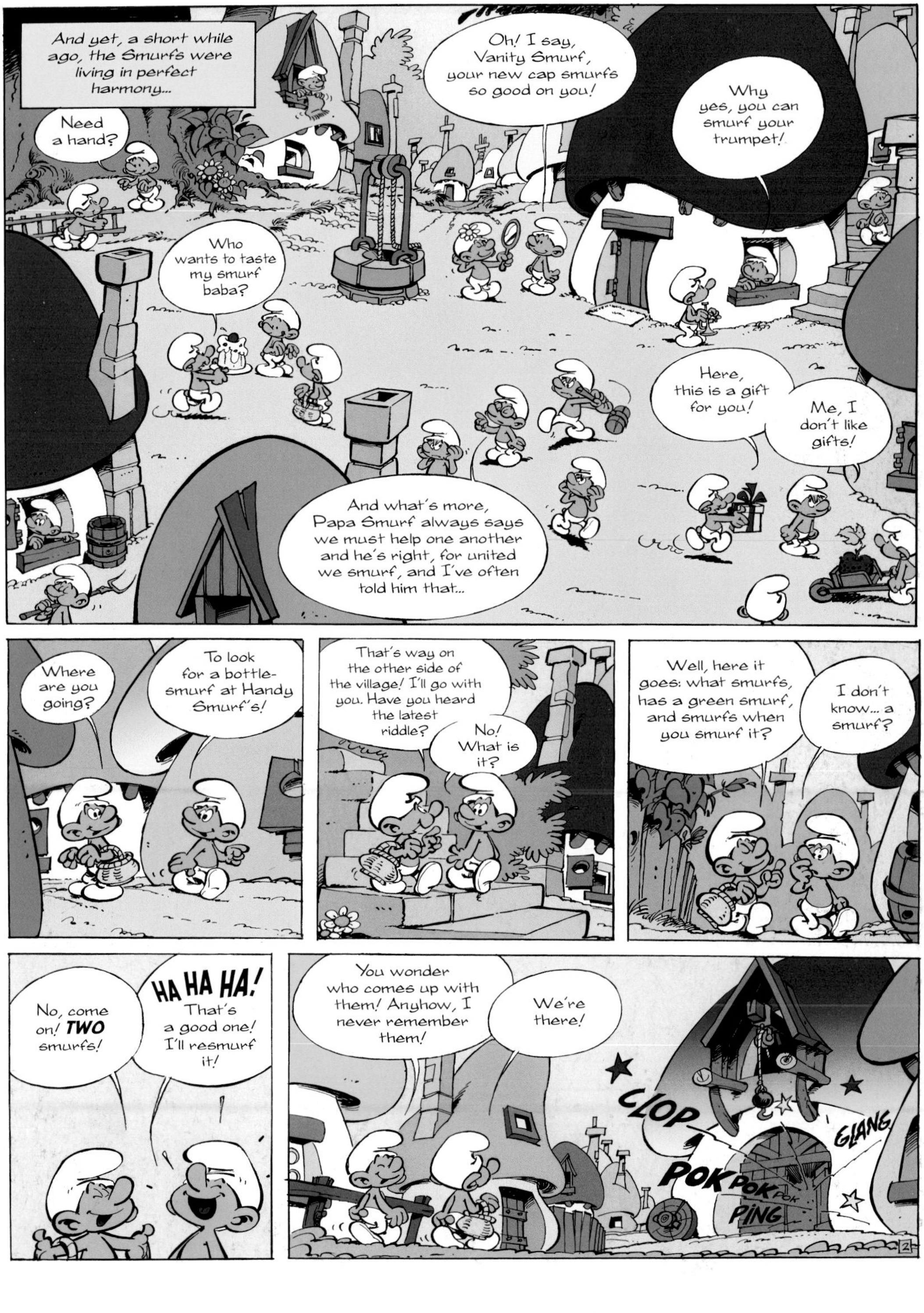
And yet, a short while ago, the Smurfs were living in perfect harmony...
Need a hand?
Oh! I say, Vanity Smurf, your new cap smurfs so good on you!
Why yes, you can smurf your trumpet!
Who wants to taste my smurf baba?
Here, this is a gift for you!
Me, I don't like gifts!
And what's more, Papa Smurf always says we must help one another and he's right, for united we smurf, and I've often told him that...
Where are you going?
To look for a bottle-smurf at Handy Smurf's!
That's way on the other side of the village! I'll go with you. Have you heard the latest riddle?
No! What is it?
Well, here it goes: what smurfs, has a green smurf, and smurfs when you smurf it?
I don't know... a smurf?
No, come on! TWO smurfs!
HA HA HA! That's a good one! I'll resmurf it!
You wonder who comes up with them! Anyhow, I never remember them!
We're there!
CLOP
CLANG
POK POK POK
PING

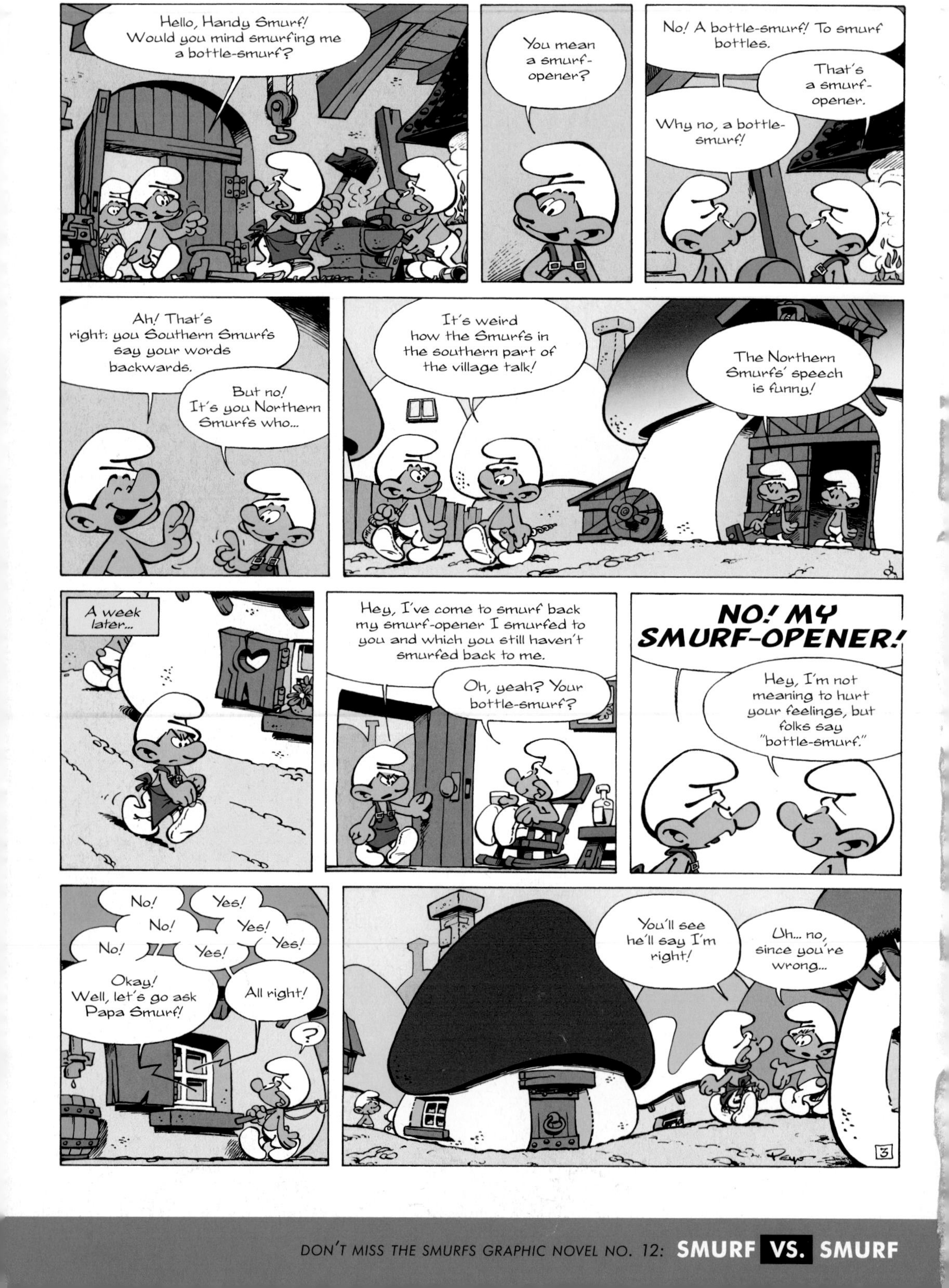
Hello, Handy Smurf! Would you mind smurfing me a bottle-smurf?
You mean a smurf-opener?
No! A bottle-smurf! To smurf bottles.
That's a smurf-opener.
Why no, a bottle-smurf!
Ah! That's right: you Southern Smurfs say your words backwards.
But no! It's you Northern Smurfs who...
It's weird how the Smurfs in the southern part of the village talk!
The Northern Smurfs' speech is funny!
A week later...
Hey, I've come to smurf back my smurf-opener I smurfed to you and which you still haven't smurfed back to me.
Oh, yeah? Your bottle-smurf?
NO! MY SMURF-OPENER!
Hey, I'm not meaning to hurt your feelings, but folks say "bottle-smurf."
No!
Yes!
No!
Yes!
No!
Yes!
Yes!
Okay! Well, let's go ask Papa Smurf!
All right!
?
You'll see he'll say I'm right!
Uh... no, since you're wrong...
3

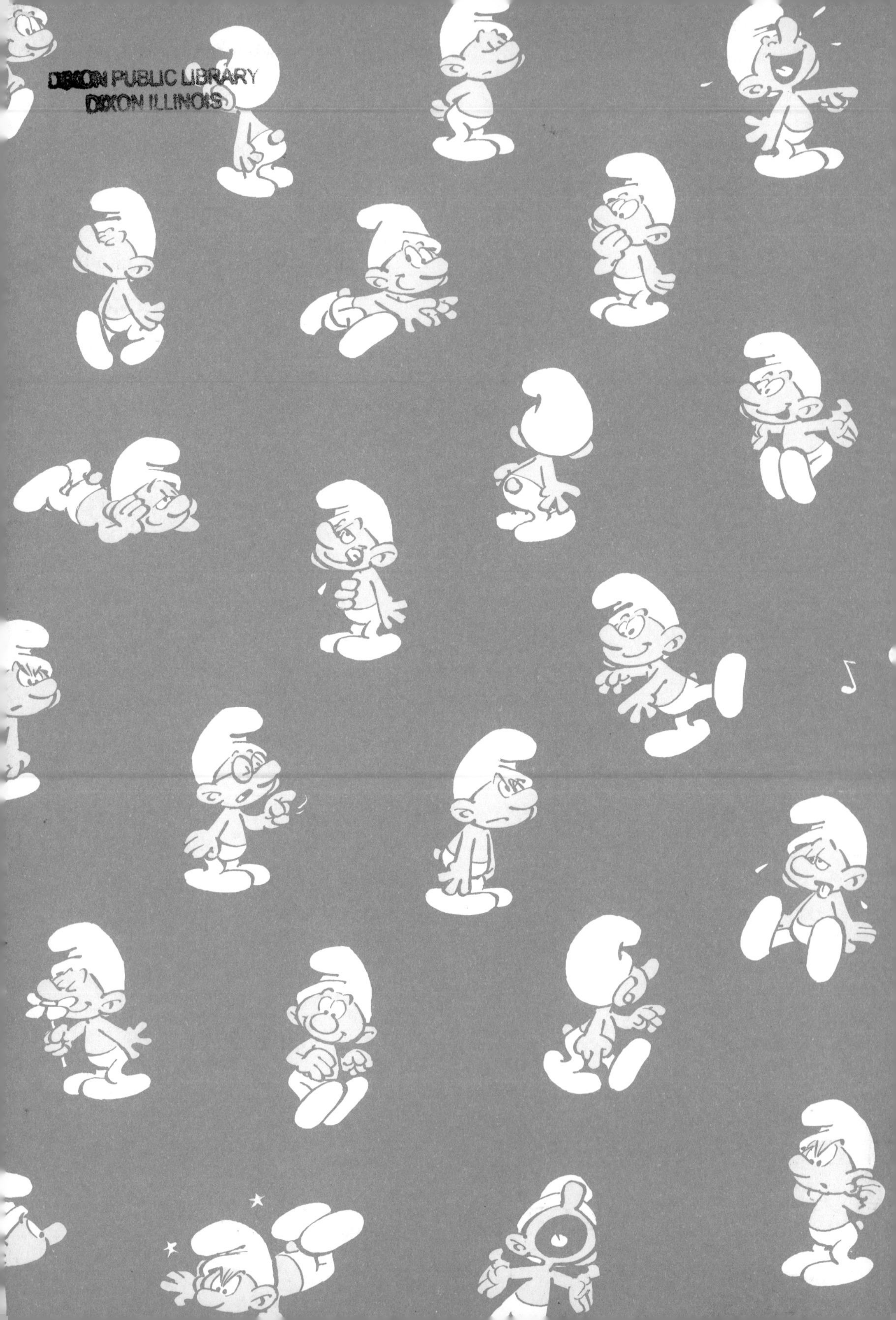